"How much do you charge for house calls?"

David's question was an angry demand, and Shelly stared at him in dismay. His barriers had gone up, and once more he was on the attack.

"Not a thing," she informed him crisply. "They're simply her friends and guests here whom your aunt thinks would benefit from my attention.

His expression turned skeptical. "Do I look like a man who was born yesterday?"

"You look like a man with a nasty, suspicious mind!"

He slowly massaged his jaw and muttered, "You certainly seem determined to stay here."

"For two months, yes." She bestowed a sugar-sweet smile on him.

"Okay, two months you want, two months you've got." As he reached the door he paused and said, "But if you're pulling any kind of a stunt, God help you!"

ELIZABETH OLDFIELD began writing professionally as a teenager after taking a mail order writing course, of all things. She later married a mining engineer, gave birth to a daughter and a son and happily put her writing career on hold. Her husband's work took them to Singapore for five years, where Elizabeth found romance novels and became hooked on the genre. Now she's a full-time writer in Scotland and has the best of both worlds—a rich family life and a career that fits the needs of her husband and children.

Books by Elizabeth Oldfield

HARLEQUIN PRESENTS

765—THE EGO TRAP
805—DRAGON MAN
901—SUNSTROKE
948—BODYCHECK
964—BACHELOR IN PARADISE
1012—BEWARE OF MARRIED MEN
1030—TOUCH AND GO
1077—QUICKSANDS
1101—LIVING DANGEROUSLY
1132—CLOSE PROXIMITY

ELIZABETH OLDFIELD

sparring partners

Harlequin Books

TORONTO • NEW YORK • LONDON
AMSTERDAM • PARIS • SYDNEY • HAMBURG
STOCKHOLM • ATHENS • TOKYO • MILAN

Harlequin Presents first edition October 1989
ISBN 0-373-11212-2

Original hardcover edition published in 1989
by Mills & Boon Limited

Printed in U.S.A.

CHAPTER ONE

IN SLOW motion Shelly swivelled, her hazel eyes travelling from the workbench with its plaster slab, to the kick-wheel, across walls of wooden shelving, to rest finally on the shiny electric kiln. As gifts went, a pottery studio had to be one of the most unusual; yet it was a gift which, in her opinion, ought never to have been made. She heaved a troubled sigh. If only Beatrice had not got it into her head to purchase the defunct delicatessen and fill it with what appeared to be every single item listed in the potters' supplies catalogue—and if only Gail had not accepted. It did not matter that since taking possession her sister had toiled hard and long and, after only six months, was selling an encouraging proportion of her wares; what mattered was that the old lady's benevolence rated as too extravagant by half!

Impatiently Shelly hooked a wayward strand of fair, silky hair behind her ear. When she had returned from attending a health seminar in Paris and discovered that a suburban property had been added to her young sister's modest collection of worldly goods, a fierce protest had been registered. It was thumbs down. She did not approve. Such over-the-top largesse must be refused. Tell her thanks, but no, thanks, she had insisted. But she was wasting her breath, for during her absence everything had been signed, sealed and delivered. Gail legally owned the terraced premises, plus contents. Nothing Shelly had said had altered anything. Her sister's argument had been that Beatrice had *needed* to help and was investing her love as much as her money. As for the donor, it did not seem to have occurred to her that others might consider her open-handedness to be rash, inflammatory or unjust.

Shelly sighed again. The transaction had provided both participants with immense pleasure, so why did she continue to fret? What was done was done. Her worries were mental masochism and served no purpose. After all, the pottery had been given and received in the utmost good faith. As she trailed her fingertips across a cluster of porcelain flower-appliquéd globes, her mind went to the trauma of three days ago. Although she had always regarded the affection which had sprung up between the old lady and her sister to be sincere and durable, it was only when Beatrice had fallen and broken her hip that the true depth of their dependency on each other had hit home.

'Please, please, let her survive,' Gail had whimpered, as she had sped to her side. She was distraught and wild-eyed, and her anguish had known no bounds.

Equally, Beatrice's relief when her young friend had arrived had been tremendous. The tears which had streamed down her cheeks as she drew the girl close had touched everyone. But the unconventional senior citizen—with her gaudy shawls and ornate straw hats, she reminded Shelly of a wrinkled flower-child—had no intention of allowing 'a cussed fracture' to get the better of *her*. The initial distress had been rapidly surmounted, and when they had visited the hospital earlier this afternoon they had found Beatrice pale but smiling—and delivering a monologue to a somewhat dazed-looking woman in the next bed. In addition to her generosity, the old lady possessed another doubtful attribute: the gift of the gab.

Shelly abandoned her thoughts and consulted her wristwatch. After leaving Beatrice she had headed for the supermarket, while Gail had kept a dental appointment. The arrangement had been that, when their respective buses deposited them at the stop outside the pottery, whoever arrived first would wait, then together they would carry the weekend shopping up the hill to the flat. Her sister had stipulated four o'clock at the latest, but it was almost four-fifteen. Perhaps she had missed the bus?

On the point of deciding to haul the grocery bags up the final stretch herself, Shelly heard the march of footsteps, followed by a creak as the street door was wrenched open.

'Hi,' she said, in smiling anticipation. 'What happened? Did the——'

Her voice faded, her smile collapsed. Instead of her sister rushing in from the sunny September afternoon, she found herself confronted by a tall, tanned, athletic-looking man in a charcoal-grey sweatshirt and cords. An unruly quiff of dark hair fell across his brow, he had a lean, intelligent face, and under black brows lurked very alert, very piercing, very blue eyes. As he strode forward to plant himself in the middle of the floor, Shelly felt a ripple of resentment. The door might not have been locked, but it had been closed, and this stranger had no right to barge in without even knocking.

'I'm sorry, this isn't a shop or a showroom. It's private property,' she informed him politely but firmly. 'However, if you wish to buy something——'

'I don't.'

The sharp rebuttal jolted her into a reassessment. The granite set of his jaw, the determination she saw in his well-cut mouth, the glitter of his gaze, identified him as a man with a mission. If he was not interested in the ceramics, then equally he had not wandered in at random to ask for directions or the time of day. Far from it, he had deliberately and rapaciously *infiltrated*.

'So what do you want?' Shelly enquired.

Eyes as coldly thorough as searchlights scanned her slim figure in natural linen blouse and matching slacks, topped by a topaz-coloured leather waistcoat.

'What do *I* want? Hasn't it been more a case of you stating what *you* want?'

'Excuse me?' she said, puzzled.

'Don't bother to act dumb. Beatrice has told me all about your . . . arrangement,' he grated, holding the word out at arm's length as though it offended him.

Her arrangement? Shelly frowned, her mind a blank, then decided a split second later that he must be referring to her treatment of the old lady's arthritis—what else? As a physiotherapist who specialised in alleviating the illness, when she had learned Beatrice was a sufferer she had offered assistance. Over the months, regular exercise sessions had produced a satisfying upsurge in her patient's state of health. Beatrice's joints were not so swollen. Beatrice could walk more easily. And Beatrice was overwhelmingly—and garrulously—grateful.

'But I've helped Mrs Wilkins,' she protested, wondering where he could find fault.

His eyes blazed blue fire. 'You've helped yourself!' Thrusting his hands into his trouser pockets, the man rocked back on his heels and assessed the studio as she had done minutes earlier—though with the difference that whereas Shelly had been uneasy, his review was downright hostile. 'Congratulations, you appear to have every last thing the hick potter could possibly need.'

'Oh, I'm not——' she began, belatedly recognising that his arrival had nothing to do with her activities but everything to do with Gail's.

'After flirting with an occult group, paying out money to bogus spiritualists, and marching in praise of a diet of ginseng and comfrey—for crying out loud,' he scythed, in a deep voice with an accent which hovered somewhere in the mid-Atlantic, 'I guess it was a natural progression for Beatrice to become a patron of the arts. She always has been a loony.'

'No, she's not!' Shelly retorted, spiritedly leaping to the defence. The poor soul was flat out in hospital, after all. 'I agree that Mrs Wilkins can be a little bit . . . eccentric, but——'

'A helluva lot eccentric. Twelve months ago her obsession was collecting dab and blob paintings, but this year—guess what?—she's financing the manufacture of——' disparaging eyes scratched over the rows of ceramic globes, plates and bowls '—pots. If Harold's aware of how his hard-earned cash is being squandered, he must be spinning in his grave.'

'Who—who are you?' she faltered, as a sudden apprehension struck. For this man to be so conversant with Beatrice's background, it followed that he must either be a friend—or a relative. Shelly shivered, chilled by the premonition that she knew his exact branch of the family tree.

'My name's David Llewellyn.'

It was the answer she had expected. The answer she had dreaded. 'You mean you're the——' Her tongue had seized up and required to be motivated again. 'The nephew? Mrs Wilkins' nephew?' she checked, in the giddy, desperate, nail-biting hope that Beatrice's circle might somehow include a second person with the same name.

He gave a terse nod. 'She's spoken about me?'

'Often.'

Beatrice had not just spoken, she had drooled. The child David had been a model of juvenile perfection, while the adult David—he was somewhere in his thirties—continued to be all things bright and beautiful, only more so. Tales of his skill as an airline pilot were legion. Fly with him and you could forget about turbulence or bumpy landings or fog. And should terrorists attempt a hijack, never worry, in two seconds he would immobilise the lot. Shelly was certain that when passengers heard that David Llewellyn occupied the flight deck, they burst into manic applause. Yet, although the old lady portrayed him as the kind of Sir Galahad every right-thinking maiden would extract eye-teeth to meet, for Shelly the subtext had read 'to be avoided at all costs'. But now he was here in the living, breathing and dangerously disapproving flesh!

'Mrs Wilkins may have made one or two errors of judgement, but she's been advised that the majority of her oils are excellent investments,' she said, sidetracking to give herself time to recover.

'Advised by whom—the chimpanzees who painted them? I guess it must have been one of them who put you in touch with her,' he grated. 'It sure as hell isn't chance that's had her mining such a rich vein of second-hand car salesmen.'

'Hold on a minute,' Shelly protested, beaming a grin intended to soothe. 'I realise that in the past Mrs Wilkins has had the odd bad experience, but you can't lump together everyone she knows and label them all as suspect.'

'No?' The room received another swift and inauspicious scrutiny. 'If you want proof that conmen—correction, conwomen—abound, then what about this place? I'd say it rates as Exhibit A.'

Indignant colour washed up her face. 'I object to that!' Shelly flared.

'Do you? I am sorry.' David Llewellyn's smile was devoid of humour. 'But even an appealing blonde with huge, innocent brown eyes and dimples isn't capable of fooling all of the people all of the time. Beatrice might remain in blissful ignorance, but I know just how the grapevine here passed on the word about an old dame who possesses a darn sight more money than sense, and that you——' he leant menacingly towards her '—Miss Gail Havers, decided to muscle in.'

'I'm not Gail Havers.'

'No?' He scowled and took a step in retreat. 'Why didn't you say?' he demanded, rubbing the back of his neck with fractious fingers.

'Because I wasn't allowed the opportunity. I'm Shelly Havers, her sister,' she said, thinking, thinking. It was imperative that she ease the situation, but how? Maybe it was expecting too much for David Llewellyn to be a friend, yet he must not be allowed to become an enemy. 'However, I know all about Gail's relationship with Mrs Wilkins,' she continued, 'and I can assure you it isn't the least bit mercenary. The pottery came out of the blue. Gail had no idea your aunt intended to set her up in business.' She gave another placatory grin. 'This idea of yours that everyone's hell-bent on lining their pockets is not only jaundiced, it's totally wrong. Gail has never——'

'Who introduced your sister to Beatrice?' David Llewellyn interrupted.

'No one. They met at an exhibition of contemporary art. It was instant rapport.'

'Yeah? How old is this sister of yours?'

'Twenty-two.'

'Instant rapport between a woman over seventy and a kid barely dry behind the ears.' His smile was as deadly as gelignite. 'You don't expect me to swallow that?'

'I don't give a damn what you swallow,' Shelly replied, a surge of annoyance overruling her desire to disarm him. 'All I know is that, whatever the age difference, Mrs Wilkins and Gail have an affinity, a close one.' Her face clouded. 'They both need someone.'

'I can imagine. And how long has this——' his lip curled '—friendship existed?'

'Almost a year.'

'So after knowing your sister for—what, less than six months?—Beatrice is persuaded to loosen the purse strings? Not much time wasted, was there?'

Shelly bit back a retort and counted to ten. OK, David Llewellyn believed nothing she had said so far, yet getting mad at him would only take her backwards, not forwards.

'I presume you've been to see Mrs Wilkins at the hospital?' she said, hoping to take some of the heat out of the confrontation.

'Just now,' he confirmed curtly. 'Her next-door neighbour passed on the news of her accident, so I've driven down from Glasgow.'

'You rushed all that way?' Shelly enquired, and was unable to conceal her disdain.

A childless widow with her two sisters living abroad, Beatrice had just one relative in the entire British Isles—this much-adored nephew. The adoration, however, was strictly one-sided. David Llewellyn might regularly fly the thousands of miles between Scotland and the States, but in the time Shelly had known Beatrice he had never once bothered to travel the four hundred which separated Scotland from South Wales. At Christmas, Easter, and on her birthday, his cards had had pride of place in the old lady's drawing-room, but of the man himself there had been no trace. Whatever the qualities his aunt might laud, common-or-garden compassion did not feature among them. Even now his response smacked of the apathetic, she thought scathingly. Beatrice had fallen on Wednesday and this was Saturday!

'The message took a while to reach me,' he said, a touch defensively, 'but when I heard what had happened, I dropped everything and came.'

'How kind.' Hazel eyes locked into blue ones. 'I imagine you thought she was going to die?'

'The possibility did cross my mind,' he replied, steadily holding her gaze. 'At Beatrice's age, complications have a nasty way of setting in. Even now——'

'Mrs Wilkins is making an excellent recovery!' Shelly objected with force.

He might not have flinched at her suggestion of Beatrice's demise, but she was not so naïve she didn't know why David Llewellyn had at last managed to stir himself. His 'tender concern' could be paraphrased as 'prospects of personal gain'. Her lips compressed. Like a vulture anticipating bones to pick over, he had arrived to check out the scene!

'Mrs Wilkins is frail and confused,' he insisted. 'She claimed she'd fractured her hip playing goddamn football,' he came back at her, when Shelly voiced a protest.

'But she *did*. She was in her garden when some boys knocked a ball over the fence. The average old lady would have handed it back but, your aunt being your aunt, she decided to kick it. As she was making the run-up, she tripped over a rake. I agree it can be tricky making sense of what Mrs Wilkins tells you at times,' she continued, as he raised despairing eyes to the ceiling, 'and perhaps more so at the moment because she's suffered a big shock to her system. But that's only because she skips from one subject to another, with no attention to past, present or future. To people who are rarely in her company——' Shelly shone a smile which was all mouth and no eyes '—Mrs Wilkins may appear to be vague but, in fact, she knows precisely what she's doing.'

David Llewellyn gave a low growl of irritation. 'Like dishing out a thirty-thousand-pound freebie to a kid who's little more than an acquaintance?'

'The studio cost just over twenty thousand, all-in.'

He tilted a sarcastic head. 'Forgive my error.'

'Earlier you called Gail a hick, but she isn't. She's a fully trained potter with a degree, and although she's young her work's strikingly mature and original,' Shelly extolled, in earnest defence. 'Her ceramics are already popular with local craft shops, and a top London department store is considering whether or not to place an order. If they do, her future will be virtually guaranteed.'

'So how soon can the family expect the twenty thousand plus to be paid back?' he enquired silkily.

'Paid back?' she echoed.

'Paid back,' he decreed.

Shelly squirmed. During endless nights of misgivings, she had imagined a scenario similar to this one. Then, his irate demands as to the whys and wherefores had been subdued by Gail's explanations and—albeit grudgingly—he had understood. Restitution had not been demanded. But the David Llewellyn in her mind's eye had been humane, open to reason and, in the end, philosophical; this one was not. Her chin lifted. She might harbour grave reservations about Beatrice's handout herself yet, when faced with such brutal opposition, she found herself determined to defend the old lady's right to have made it.

'The pottery was an outright gift,' she informed him.

'Something which is wheedled, inveigled and cadged falls a long way outside that description!'

Shelly's backbone stiffened. She stood to attention. 'The pottery was *not* cadged,' she declared, nostrils flaring.

'Cut out the hurt dignity,' he jeered, 'and try telling the truth for once.'

'I am!'

'I've had it with people taking advantage of my relations,' he muttered, as though she had never spoken. 'It's not that long ago since Jessica was duped, and she is the gentlest, kindest, most welcoming——' He broke off to frown and run a hand through his thick, dark hair. 'She never deserved to be treated like that.'

Jessica, Shelly knew, was Beatrice's youngest sister. Another widow, she ran a hotel on a small island in the Caribbean. But if David Llewellyn failed to jump through hoops on Mrs Wilkins' account, his attitude made it plain he did care about this other aunt—and deeply. No longer the marauding heavyweight who had stormed in with fists raised, he was now dismayed by his thoughts, now awash with concern.

'What happened?' Shelly asked.

'This guy and his wife came out to stay at Severney Great House and——' He glared as though she had tricked him into confidences against his will. 'Never mind. When does your sister recompense my family?' he demanded.

Shelly stood firm. 'I don't consider she needs to.'

'*You* don't consider?' A dark brow arched. 'Then I assume you make the decisions around here? I should have guessed as much,' he carried on, allowing her no chance to reply. 'It'd need to be a very hardboiled kid of twenty-two who would select, soften and fleece an old woman single-handed. So, big sister directs operations?'

She shook a wondering head. He made life sound like something out of an old Edward G. Robinson movie—all fiendish plots and do-'em-down collaborations.

'You've got it wrong. There isn't, and never has been, an "operation".'

'Wrong or not, the bottom line is that the money must be repaid. Soon.' He flexed his shoulders, the fighter once more. 'If it isn't, then the family will have no other option than to resort to the law.'

'The—the law?' Shelly stammered, gaping at him as if transfixed.

'Befuddled old widow defrauded of thousands. It'd be an open and shut case.'

'But Mrs Wilkins isn't befuddled and she hasn't been defrauded! She made a deliberate, clear-thinking decision to provide Gail with her own studio. She located the premises, she ordered the equipment, she did *everything*,' Shelly gabbled, hearing in her mind the tramp of feet along stone corridors, the turn of a key, the ominous clang of a solid metal door. '*She* doesn't want the money back.'

'You reckon Harold Wilkins spent his life working all the hours God sent on your sister's account?' he gibed.

'No,' she was forced to admit, 'but——'

'You deny that morally that twenty thousand ought to stay with his widow as he intended and should subsequently be passed on to the family?' David Llewellyn demanded.

Shelly gnawed uncertainly at her lip. The questions he raised were ones she had already asked herself, but she had never come up with foolproof answers then.

'Mrs Wilkins is allowed to spend her money how she likes,' she pointed out.

'You'd advocate her acting the Lady Bountiful all the way down to the poverty line?'

It was another punch between the eyes.

'Of course not,' she said, beginning to feel battered.

'So would you kindly advise your sister that she's to sell up and make retribution?' He lined up another blow. 'By the end of the year.'

Mentally she steadied herself. 'Mrs Wilkins wouldn't want Gail to do that.'

'If I explain how your sister's had second thoughts, she'll understand.'

Shelly glowered. Grief, but he was smug. Unfortunately, Beatrice's hero-worship meant he could also be right.

'But if Gail did cease trading, all she'd get for the fixtures and fittings would be a knockdown price,' she demurred. 'Also, the property had been for sale for more than two years before Mrs Wilkins came along, so the chances of disposing of it quickly for the same sum have to be remote. It would be difficult, if not impossible, to recoup the whole twenty thousand.'

'Then you'd need to concoct a way of making up the shortfall.'

She stared at him. 'How?'

'A smart cookie like you must have some skills you can market,' David Llewellyn said scornfully. The piercing blue eyes undertook a leisurely—and disturbing—tour of her body. 'It's astonishing what a come-hither look and a twitch of a hip can achieve.'

'What's that supposed to mean?' Shelly demanded.

'Use your imagination.'

Fiery circles flushed her cheeks. 'You're suggesting I become a—a hooker?'

'I'm suggesting you and your sister refund my aunt—in full,' he snapped. 'You have a month to work out a repayment package. I'd like to have your proposals in writing. Pass the letter to Beatrice, she knows where to reach me.' He took a step towards the door, then turned. 'She has enough to bother about with her fractured hip, so we'll keep this private for the time being. OK?'

She blinked. Everything was happening too fast. 'Er—OK.'

The watch strapped to his broad wrist received a glance, and he scowled. 'I should have been on the road back to Glasgow an hour ago.'

'You're not staying on to see Mrs Wilkins again?' she enquired tartly.

'I'm afraid I can't spare the time.'

I'm afraid you can't be bothered now that you know she's going to survive, Shelly interpreted caustically. As he powered for the exit, she went after him. She might be battered, but she was not ready to be counted out.

'Mr Llewellyn——' she began in protest.

'I expect to hear from you within the month,' he overrode her, 'but if I don't——' his voice became a menacing purr '—you and your sister are going to find yourselves in big, *big* trouble.'

'Mr Llewellyn——' Shelly said again.

He had gone.

'If you're accused of extortion or whatever it's called, are you put in prison until the trial?' Gail fidgeted unhappily with her ponytail. 'Even if you insist you're innocent, are you kept there on remand?'

'Look, David Llewellyn had come straight from learning about the pottery, and his anger was a knee-jerk response,' Shelly avowed.

'So tomorrow he'll telephone and say everything's fine by him?' her sister asked, her face brightening as her spirits zoomed.

'He might.'

'But he might not.' The doubts had been recognised. 'I could spread the word that I might be putting the studio up for sale—very discreetly—just to see if there'd be any interest,' the girl suggested.

Shelly's eyes went to the white envelope with green and gold insignia which was propped up on the mantelpiece.

'And pass up the chance every potter in the UK would kill for?'

After the bad news had come the good. A first order from the department store for porcelain plates had been waiting at the flat, with confirmation that subsequent deliveries would be required over the next few months.

'I'd hate to tell them no,' Gail sighed.

'You don't need to.' Shelly raised her coffee-cup and grinned. 'Here's to my kid sister, who's going places.'

'But suppose David Llewellyn *does* start legal proceedings?' the girl fretted, when cups had been clinked.

'No matter how fantastic she believes him to be, Beatrice isn't going to perjure herself. She's going to tell it how it actually happened. Sooner or later, he'll realise that and——'

Again her sister soared from despair to wild optimism. 'Then we're safe?' she interrupted eagerly.

The plural had been unconscious, yet was meant. Childhood dilemmas had always been tackled together—with Shelly taking charge, offering solutions, comforting—and now, whenever problems surfaced, Gail took her involvement for granted.

'For the moment—I believe so.'

'You don't think that when it becomes obvious we're not going to be browbeaten, he'll try and talk Beatrice into demanding the money back?'

'And risk putting himself in her bad books? Never. As long as Beatrice is around I don't see that there's anything he can do.' Shelly hesitated. 'Though if she should disappear from the scene——'

'Bea isn't going to do that, not for years and years,' came the stout declaration.

'I hope you're right, but no one lasts for ever,' she warned. 'David Llewellyn mentioned her brush with the spiritualists——'

'The ones who tricked her?'

'Yes, and if he slotted you in the same bracket and Beatrice wasn't there, it might be difficult to set the record straight. Looked at from the outside, you *could* have coaxed her to part with her money. How on earth would we prove that you didn't?'

Gail pouted. 'I don't know why he's making such a fuss. As far as Bea's concerned, the twenty thousand is peanuts. Well, nearly.'

'It's a sizeable chunk to you and me,' Shelly protested. 'And a *very* sizeable chunk to someone who's determined to believe it's been swindled.'

The girl rested a glum elbow on the tale. 'Suppose I phone David Llewellyn and have a bash at getting him to see reason? I could say that once I'm established I'd be willing to pay the money back, in instalments. It'll take years and it isn't at all what Beatrice has in mind, but——'

'He wouldn't be interested. He wants the lump sum returned, pronto.'

'He can't have it!' Gail's belligerence was short-lived. 'So what do we do—nothing?'

Shelly frowned. David Llewellyn was not the type to take kindly to having his demands ignored. Indeed, if the situation went untended, he could build up a perilous amount of resentment.

'If we could, it'd be wise to make a gesture of goodwill,' she mused. 'Do something which would show that, although the twenty thousand isn't being returned, it is appreciated. Convince him we're not the sharks he imagines.'

'How do we do that?' her sister enquired.

'I wish I knew.' She took a drink of coffee. 'He was so *anti*,' she complained.

'He must have some finer feelings, some soft spots.'

'I only noticed one—a fondness for his Aunt Jessica. Hang on,' she said, grappling with an idea which had suddenly surfaced. 'If only I could——'

'Could what?' Gail prodded, when Shelly sighed and shook her head.

'You remember how Beatrice has talked about her sister also suffering with arthritis, and how she's written to her about my exercises, and how Mrs Severney has replied saying she wishes she could take a course herself? I was thinking——'

'That she can, if you go out to the Caribbean!' Gail completed, in triumph. 'And when he learns how you've helped her, David Llewellyn'll be so grateful, he won't mind about Beatrice giving me the pottery. He'll still mind,' the girl adjusted, hearing his capitulation sound too glib, 'but he'll accept it.'

'Maybe,' Shelly agreed. 'But how can I possibly treat Mrs Severney?' she appealed. 'A course would take two months minimum, and——'

'You've yet to have this year's annual leave, and there's a fortnight you never took from last, right?' Gail demanded. 'Couldn't you beg another couple of weeks on an unpaid basis?'

'It wouldn't be easy, but—— Have you any idea how expensive all this would be?' she demanded.

'I'll sell the gold necklace and earrings Mum left me,' her sister said, at speed. 'Say you'll do it, Shelly, *please*. You've always hankered for faraway places, and it'd be mostly a holiday, and it'd get David Llewellyn off our backs. We don't want to live in constant fear of the guy, do we?'

'It would be a bit harrowing,' she admitted.

'So you'll go to the Caribbean? For me?'

Shelly weighed up the pros and cons, then grinned. 'OK, though we'll split the cost,' she insisted, through an avalanche of thanks and hugs. 'I'll ask Beatrice for Mrs Severney's number, then if—when—she agrees, I'll clear my absence with the surgery and book the first available flight.' Her brown eyes gleamed. 'With luck, what's happening won't filter through to Scotland for a while, which'll suit me fine. I'd much prefer to spring it on David Llewellyn.'

'He does expect to hear from us within a month,' Gail reminded her.

'Don't worry, I'll write and explain—once I've assessed how much I'll be able to do for his aunt.' All of a sudden, Shelly frowned. 'You know, there's one thing more than anything else which really bugs me.'

'What's that?'

'How throughout our entire conversation he continually referred to "the family". The *family* expect the money to be paid back. The *family* will resort to the law. David Llewellyn might be Beatrice's blue-eyed boy,' she derided, 'but he had neither the grace—nor the guts—to own up to being her sole heir!'

CHAPTER TWO

SHELLY had taken the travel agent's claim that she would transfer to Nevis in less time than it took the jumbo jet's passengers to clear Customs and check into their Antiguan hotels with a massive pinch of salt. But he had told the truth. People travelling onward to the tiny jewel of an island had been requested to disembark from the London flight first. At the edge of the tarmac the five of them—herself and two couples—had been greeted by a cheerful and efficient coloured girl. Within minutes their suitcases were identified, loaded on to a trolley, and they were being led across to a neat white plane emblazoned with the Hawk-Air slogan in cerise and gold. As the luggage was stowed, they were offered glasses of champagne or iced fresh orange, then supplied with fragrant towels to wipe hands and faces. The charter airline had to be commended. It was impeccable service with a smile.

When the pilot, a jovial bearded American, suggested she might like to sit beside him in the cockpit, Shelly grabbed at the chance. This was her first time in such a small plane and despite spending most of the day in the air already, she remained eager for experiences. Not much later they were high above a sea of pale turquoise, watching fishing-boats, the size of toys, bob on the waves. A cruise-ship gleamed expensively white in the sunshine. She spotted an atoll, fringed with palms. In the distance an island shimmered among the haze: a wooded mountain rising skyward, a line of surf lapping the coast. Excitement brought a smile. This was the stuff from which dreams were made and, for the moment, *why* she had come to the West Indies ceased to matter.

As the pilot removed his headphones, the balding, middle-aged man behind tapped him on the shoulder.

'I imagine that must be Nevis?' he said, gesturing ahead.

'Correct, but the name's pronounced "*Nee*vis". See how the mountain's capped with mist? The story goes that when Columbus sighted the island he named it *"Nuestra Señora de las Nieves"*, Our Lady of the Snows, and Nevis derived from that. Where are you folks staying?' he enquired.

'At Severney Great House,' the balding man said, introducing himself and his partner as Mr and Mrs Shepherd.

'I am, too,' grinned Shelly.

'We're booked in at the Creole Beach,' the woman in the rear contributed in a strong German accent.

The pilot provided more facts, answered more questions and, as they reached the island, pointed out first the German couple's hotel and then the Great House. Eagerly Shelly peered down. Beatrice had greeted news of her trip with wide smiles and a mass of information, but this had been so hotchpotched, it had left her not knowing *what* to expect. To her relief, the view from the air was encouraging. In the midst of trim lawns stood a solid cut-stone building, tinged golden by the sun. The front of the house was served by a drive which wound up from the road, while the back faced the ocean down a broad grassy avenue. On either side of the avenue were acres of palms, and among them she picked out small pastel-painted cottages.

'I believe Severney was built as a sugar plantation homestead in the eighteenth century?' Shelly enquired.

The pilot nodded. 'That's right.'

'And later the crop was coconuts?'

'Right again.'

'A well-read young lady,' Mr Shepherd praised. He had a weakness for the prettier members of the fairer sex, privately calling them 'life's enhancers', and this girl, with her petal-smooth complexion, glossy shoulder-length hair and infectious smile, would brighten anyone's day. 'I expect you know all about the Great House being furnished with antiques?'

She laughed, recognising a blank page in Beatrice's verbal dossier. 'Not a thing.'

'Jessica Severney is one of nature's hostesses,' the pilot said. 'She runs her hotel as though it's a private country house and the visitors are old friends. Not only does she dine with her guests most nights, but she goes out of her way to ensure everyone has a wonderful time. And you will.'

Five minutes' later, they touched down. Smiling goodbye to the American, Shelly clambered from the cockpit and looked around. The airport was miniature, just a landing-strip in a field with a few cabins close by for Immigration and Customs. She put on her sunglasses, hung her travel-bag over her shoulder, and went with the others to claim her luggage. The formalities did not take long, and soon she and the Shepherds were piling into the taxi which was to carry them the twelve miles to their destination.

Edged by lush undergrowth, the narrow road snaked sometimes close to the shoreline, dallying with silver sand beaches, and sometimes twisted away. Through a village of weathered clapboard houses they sped, where chickens pecked in the dirt and children with dazzling white grins hung over balconies and waved. They passed a man on a donkey, glimpsed enormous black pigs rooting for food, caught sight of a tumbledown windmill covered in blossom. Shelly grinned. With work her first priority, she did not exactly fit the 'guest' label, yet she still believed the pilot's claim. How could anyone fail to have a wonderful time on a tropical island?

Severney Great House looked even more impressive at ground level than it had done from above. Constructed with both the occasional earth tremor and the climate in mind, the sturdy, closed-in ground floor accommodated a spacious reception suite, kitchens and ancillary offices, while a broad flight of exterior stone steps led to the airier upper level. Here, so the plump black woman who greeted them explained, they would find the bar, lounge and dining-room with its broad veranda.

'Mrs Severney's left a message,' she smiled, when Shelly identified herself. 'Her sincere apologies for not being here to welcome you, but she's had to attend an unexpected meeting. However, she hopes you'll settle yourself in and she's looking forward to seeing you tomorrow morning around ten o'clock.' The woman handed over a key. 'If you go outside you'll find Wellington in the pick-up. He'll run you down to your cottage.'

Hot, sticky and suddenly tired, Shelly was grateful for a lift; even more so when she realised that the distance between the Great House and her accommodation was near enough a quarter of a mile. The cottage, a pretty lemon-washed building decorated with delicate gingerbread, turned out to be semi-detached, and the youth indicated the blue-glossed door on the left. With unmistakable pride, he showed her through the sitting-room with its floral sofa and chairs, the straw- and white-coloured bedroom, the streamlined bathroom.

'Happy hour's six until seven, and dinner's at eight,' he explained, in relaxed, drawn-out Caribbean vowels. 'Make your way over whenever you're ready.' He scanned the sky, where grey clouds were rolling in from the sea. 'I wouldn't leave it too late. We could be in for a spot of rain.' He jabbed his finger towards a line of lamps set among the grass. 'Those'll light your path. See you later,' he grinned, and jumped back into the cab.

When she had unpacked, Shelly stripped off her clothes and stretched out on the bed. Soon she would shower, but first she must cool off. For a minute or two she watched the fan which circled in the ceiling, and then...

In the first moment of awakening, she did not know where she was. Shelly panicked. Her heart banged. Why the obsidian black? What was that roaring noise? Then, with a nervous laugh at her foolishness, where, why and what were recognised. She was in the cottage, waking up from an unexpected nap, slapbang in the middle of a tropical storm. Darkness had fallen, and the roar comprised a combination of rain on the roof with the pound of surf on the nearby shore. She fumbled at the lamp on the bedside-table, but despite a click nothing happened. Sighing, she arose and, feeling her way inch by unfamiliar inch, made it to the door. No joy with the switch there, either. Shelly blew out a breath to raise limp straggles of hair from her brow. Dark or not, rain or not, the bedroom was stifling. Then she realised that the ceiling fan had ceased to twirl. Among her meanderings she remembered that Beatrice had mentioned erratic electricity, so presumably there had been a power cut? An inspection through the mosquito-netted window revealed inky black all around with a speckle of lights in the distance—of course, the Great House would be equipped with an emergency generator.

Uncertain how long she had slept, but aware of being hungry, Shelly was grateful to find her watch's luminous hands stood at seven-fifteen. Forty-five minutes allowed ample time in which to shower, dress, and go over for dinner. Yet as she located the candles she had seen in a drawer, set them around the bathroom, later traipsed with them into the bedroom, found her clothes in the gloom and returned to the bathroom to make up her face, that ample time dwindled. At five to eight, she fastened a mackintosh over her ivory silk blouse and pencil-slim skirt, and looked hastily around for a rainhood. Drawers were riffled through, her case re-opened. Come eight o'clock she was still searching. At five past, she grabbed a plastic supermarket carrier she had used to wrap shoes and plonked that over her head instead. Hardly *haute couture*, more like comic cuts, but who was going to see her scuttling through the trees in the dark?

The trouble was, when Shelly blew out the candles and opened the door, the dark looked excessively dark. Monstrous black clouds covered the moon. A groaning wind swayed the trees. Rain pelted down. The Caribbean had turned hostile. Fixing her eyes on the hotel lights, she told herself she did not have far to go *really*. She locked up, pocketed the key and positioned her makeshift hat.

'Oops!' she squeaked, when her shoe skidded on the wet grass.

Shelly gulped in a breath, warned herself to take more care, and, as the wind snatched at her mac and the rain lashed her legs, walked on. She shuddered. She did not like forcing her way through the pitch black, did not like it at all. She felt so alone. Like the last person left on earth. A whine of wind had her glancing up at the palm trees. Who would have thought they could bend so low, then whiplash? Who would have imagined that their great leafy, tossing heads could look so much like dreadlocks shaking out dire warnings? But that was what this fearfulness was—*imagination*. Trees were only trees, and all she had to do was reach the Great House. A raindrop trickled down her neck. Or should she? Admittedly she had gone about a third of the way, yet did braving the elements make much sense? Wouldn't she do better to scrub the idea of dinner and return to the security of home base?

Torn, Shelly cast a look over her shoulder. Her gaze narrowed. Back in the vicinity of her cottage, among the widely spaced palms, shone a small circle of yellow light. She was not alone. Someone with an umbrella over their head and a torch in their hand was following her. Someone whom, from their height and purposeful stride, appeared aggressively male. Her pursuer would be one of the guests... wouldn't he? At the cough of distant thunder, she jumped. Thunder always disturbed her. A billowy feeling of vulnerability disturbed her, too.

Did she wait for the man to catch up, or carry on walking ahead? Keep ahead, Shelly decided. Keep her distance. After all, she had no proof he was a guest. She could not recall seeing fences, so presumably anyone could wander on to the

Severney property. Anyone, like a mugger, a murderer, a psychopath! Wrapping the bag tighter around her ears, she hurried off again towards the hotel lights.

'Hold on!' called the person behind.

She pretended she had not heard. The wind and rain had almost carried the voice off anyway, so if someone did dash indoors seconds after her and complain of being ignored, she had a good excuse. Shelly glanced behind. The yellow circle was bobbing up and down. The man had begun to jog! His desire to catch up at all costs struck her as peculiar, verging on the ominous, and in reflex she began jogging, too. Better to be safe than sorry. She had not travelled all this way to the Caribbean to be mown down on her very first night.

Another call, and the thud of feet on the wet ground filled her with dismay. The man, whoever he was, must be fit, for the progress he made was dramatic. Yard by slip-sliding yard, the distance between them diminished. What would he do when he reached her? As the drum of headlines about 'body of blonde discovered' beat in her head, Shelly jogged harder. One dripping palm was circumvented, and another. Her skirt rode up above her knees, her sandals squelched, but she did not care. All she cared about was evasion. Please stop him, she begged some unknown deity. Please tire him out. Please make him fall. But it was she who fell, or who would have done if, at the last moment, harsh fingers had not bitten into her arm and kept her upright.

'Aren't you being a little bit stupid?' panted someone from behind the torch.

Shelly blinked, panting herself and blinded by the light. The beam cast eerie, jagged shadows, emphasising the stretch of the man's shirt across his chest, the sharp edge to his jaw, his straight black brows. His expression was severe. She had seen friendlier Count Dracula masks. What was he doing, skulking around in the trees on such a wicked night? she wondered, squinting against the glare. Why set up a chase? And why exhibit this steely determination to detain her? Mind ajangle, she attempted to discern reasons. Then he moved his shoulders, and his stance took on a ruthlessly sexual dimension. He seemed all muscle, all male, all menacing. Shelly's stomach hollowed. She knew exactly why he had chased her. Knew exactly why she was being detained.

'Stupid, yes?' he demanded.

To have been snared by him? She was. She was. If she could have spoken she would have agreed, but her brain had severed communication with her tongue.

'My God!' he exclaimed, suddenly bending closer.

What this betokened, Shelly did not discover, for as he had lurched forward so her fear had unravelled into sheer animal terror. Loosening a hand from the carrier bag hat, she executed a fast and furious karate chop and dashed the torch from his grasp. Taken by surprise, the man scuffled for it, and, in the upheaval, his umbrella also went adrift.

As basic language filled the air, Shelly turned and fled. She sprinted alongside a tennis court, raced past flowerbeds, scooted across the wet-slicked surface of the lawn. How she stayed upright was a miracle. In a surge of malicious strength, the wind whooshed down and snatched away her hat, but her pace never faltered. She preferred to be wet than caught! Summoning up every last ounce of effort and running at full bat, she flung herself towards the sanctuary offered by the Great House. Near, nearer, a scuttle up the stone steps, *there*.

Lights glowed golden on the netted-in veranda and voices murmured close by. She slumped to a standstill. Safe at last! Gulping in deep breaths, Shelly turned to examine the darkness. The wind continued to savage the palms, the rain poured down, but of the man there was neither sight nor sound.

A handkerchief served as a mop, then she went indoors. The lounge and bar stood empty; everyone else had gone into dinner. Shelly hung up her mac, squeezed water from the rat's tails which now did duty as hair, and tugged and straightened in an effort to make herself presentable. After a minute or two, she ventured through an archway. Elegant with wood-panelled walls and crimson brocade curtains, the dining-room contained a cluster of candlelit tables. Most of the thirty or so guests were dining in couples, though she noticed three four-somes and a larger group around a table in the centre. A waitress in a long peasant dress and with a muslin scarf knotted around her head came over.

'Would you like to sit here?' she suggested, indicating the only vacant table, one set for two in a shadowy corner. 'Or there's a place to spare at the big table.'

'This'll be fine, thanks,' Shelly said, and slid gratefully into her seat.

On any other evening she would have been happy to dine alongside others—and Mr Shepherd had smiled across from the group—but for now she preferred to be alone and inconspicuous. Time was needed in which to dry out, recover and take stock. She read the menu, ordered conch chowder followed by kingfish baked in prawn sauce, and helped herself to a roll from the basket. What did she do, report the incident and demand the police be contacted? Granted, nothing had actually *happened*, but——

A door slammed, a stride rapped out, and Shelly looked up to find her pursuer stood beneath the arch. Long legs planted apart and chest ferociously heaving, he was scanning the room. Her startled glance became a prolonged goggle of incredulity. The man who had chased her was... David Llewellyn! But why wasn't he in Scotland? Why had he come to Nevis? Could his presence be a long-shot coincidence, or had one of his aunts told him about her visit?

The questions gibbering in her head petered out as his gaze reached her corner. Shelly swallowed hard. The eyes which met hers accused her of every sin under the sun, and understandably for, if she was damp around the edges, David Llewellyn had undergone a drenching. Rain-spattered trousers clung to his thighs. His shirt resembled a damp rag. Rivulets ran from his dark hair. His arrival had caused everyone to pause simultaneously, and for a long, still moment—a minute, an hour, a year?—you could have heard the proverbial pin drop. The silence was broken when the waitress grinned, spoke to him, and handed over two large linen napkins. As he set about blotting himself, interest faded and the buzz of conversation resumed.

He had soaked up the worst when a buxom redhead in skintight violet and silver lamé called from the centre table, 'Yoo-hoo, Davie!'

He turned in her direction and gave a nod of acknowledgement. 'Good evening, Pearl.'

He intended to join the woman—thank goodness. Shelly sagged with relief. The killer of a look had been enough. His recriminations had ended there. She was not about to be taken to task—not this minute. But thanks and relief proved premature, for David Llewellyn ignored the redhead's eagerly beckoning finger and instead appeared beside *her*.

'I apologise. I made a mistake. But you looked different in the torchlight,' Shelly said, the words spilling out of her. 'Kind of weird——'

'Thanks.'

'—so I didn't recognise you. Also, I'm new to the Caribbean and not used to tropical surroundings. And I guess a full day of travelling has strung me up. Being out in the dark gave me the jitters, so when I saw you coming after me, and you shouted and you began to run, I thought—I thought——'

'You thought I intended to rape you?' he completed, when she stumbled.

Her smile was strained and brightly apologetic. 'Well . . . yes.'

His mouth took on a wry twist. 'No one can accuse you of being unimaginative.'

'Well . . . no,' Shelly was compelled to agree.

Tall, dark and undeniably virile, David Llewellyn was not the kind of man with whom most women would be willing to settle for a platonic relationship—at least, not for long. He would have no need to seek his kicks through preying on lone females. On the contrary, he probably had problems with lone females preying on *him*.

'However, if such an act did appeal,' he continued, his voice clipped and sharp, 'I would not choose to commit it in the pouring rain.' His back to the room, he grasped the edge of the table and leant towards her. 'Neither would I choose you as my victim!'

Shelly felt the blood heat her face. 'I'm sorry.'

'Sorry I'm not going to rape you?' he enquired, with heavy vitriol. 'I'd have thought you would have been grateful.'

'I am. I mean—Mr Llewellyn, when I turned and saw a figure near my cottage——'

'It happens to be my cottage, too.'

'You occupy the other half?' she bleated. It got worse and worse. He was not only on the same island at the same hotel, but he slept on the other side of the wall! 'I never heard any noises,' she said weakly.

'I heard you. Or, to be more exact, I heard the door being closed, followed by a shriek.'

Shelly fed him a tentative smile. 'My foot slipped.'

'Bad luck,' he responded grittily. 'I looked out and, to misquote the poem, "through the jungle very softly, saw a shadow flitting". The shadow appeared in need of help, but as I'd just emerged from the shower I decided to throw on a few clothes before I rushed out on my errand of mercy.' He glanced down. 'A foolish move.'

'I'll pay for everything to be laundered, dry-cleaned, whatever,' she offered. She looked across to the big table where the redhead continued to ogle him. 'Please, do go and join your friend. I regret you've been soaked, but——' much as his scowl condemned her, Shelly refused to accept the entire blame '—how was I supposed to know you were Rescue Unlimited?'

'Common sense?' he rasped, steering a damp wedge of hair from his eyes. He yanked out a chair and sat opposite her. 'And I'll dine with you.' There was a pause before he added laconically, 'If I may?'

Shelly's heart fell. As at the pottery, he had been picking off punches, jabbing and counter-jabbing, but the last thing she wanted right now was another bout of fisticuffs.

'By all means,' she said, aware that a ten-decibel *no* would fail to deter him. A moment later the waitress appeared with a steaming bowl of chowder and the menu for her companion. 'Mr Llewellyn——' Shelly began, when his choice had been made.

'David,' he said automatically, then glowered as though granting her permission to use his first name could have been rash to the point of folly.

She fastened on a polite smile. 'David, why are you in Nevis?'

'What the hell are you doing here?' he demanded at the same moment. Silence. She waited. He glared. 'OK, I'll go first,' he said impatiently. He broke open a bread roll. 'Although Antigua's my home, I stay at the Great House whenever it fits in with the Hawk-Air schedule.'

'Hawk-Air?'

'Ralph, the guy who must have flown you over, and I are in partnership.'

'Hawk-Air is your company?' she said, in amazement.

He nodded. 'At the start Ralph and I ran the show between us; now we've advanced to employing a couple of other pilots.'

'But I—I thought you worked in Scotland?' Shelly faltered. A line appeared between her brows. 'Mrs Wilkins tells tales about you living in a converted barn on the banks of the Clyde.'

'I did, until three years ago.' His smile was sardonic. 'Don't I remember you saying something about Beatrice paying no attention to past, present or future?'

'You drove down from Glasgow to see her,' she protested, sipping her soup.

'I was there to pick up spare aircraft parts. The Caribbean's off the beaten track, so sometimes there are delays,' he explained, 'and if a crisis occurs we're forced to collect items ourselves.'

'From so far away?'

'From so far away.' Irritably he plucked at his shirt, lifting the wet cotton which had plastered itself to his chest. 'Businesswise it couldn't have been a worse time, and as Beatrice had said she'd be visiting here at Christmas I deliberately made no plans to see her. It was supposed to be an in-and-out trip. Then her neighbour telephoned Jessica to say she'd fallen, and Jessica telephone Ralph, and Ralph telephoned around Scotland, and——'

'You dropped everything and came,' Shelly completed, acknowledging that, no matter how determined he might be to inherit his aunt's every last penny, he was not entirely the neglectful reprobate she had imagined.

'Would you care for some wine?' David asked, as she finished her chowder. He indicated the crystal decanter. 'Jessica serves good vintages.'

'No, thanks.'

'Being hunted down, as you thought, can't have been pleasant——'

'It wasn't,' Shelly agreed, wondering if this could be construed as an apology.

'—so a glass might help steady your nerves.'

'I understood brandy was the nerve-steadier? But I don't drink alcohol.'

'Never?'

'Never ever,' she stated firmly, but when curiosity showed in the narrowing of his eyes she realised she had been *too* firm. A mental note was made to to use a lighter touch in future. 'Drinking isn't against my religion or anything, it's just that I prefer to keep a clear head,' she added, with an oh, so casual shrug.

'And your wits about you? Very wise.' He filled his own glass. 'I've told you how I come to be here; now it's your turn.'

She sat straighter. Writing a letter was one thing, explaining face to face was another. Shelly sighed. If only she had not been responsible for his drenching. If only she had not already aroused his anger. If only his presence was not such a shock. Words were painstakingly chosen, but as her lips parted it was David who began to speak.

'Beatrice chattered on about the Great House and you thought how nice it'd be to have a holiday in the Caribbean free of charge?' he suggested.

'Free of charge?' she echoed.

'Sorry, sweetface——' a streak of hard steel had entered his voice '—living off the fat of Jessica's land, then scarpering at the crack of dawn, is much too copycat.'

Shelly looked at him in confusion. 'I don't know what you're talking about.'

'Try the sculptor and his wife who came out here. A couple Beatrice had praised to high heaven. A couple she considered her dear friends!'

Her brow furrowed. 'These are the people you mentioned at the pottery? The ones who swindled Mrs Severney?'

'Dead right. Beatrice didn't tell you how her chums sneaked off on the ferry to St Kitts early one morning, leaving a bill for three weeks' luxury board and lodging behind them?' The delivery of kingfish for two with side-plates of vegetables forced him to pause, but when the waitress had gone he continued, 'It seems you didn't come properly briefed. First, you don't know I'm here, then it turns out your scam's second-hand.' Contemptuous blue eyes picked holes in her like twin ice-axes. 'Not your day, is it?'

Shelly took a steadying breath. Being in this man's company was like taking a crash course in cynicism.

'There is no scam, as you call it,' she said quietly. 'And actually I shall be in Nevis for two months.'

CHAPTER THREE

'OVER my dead body!'

'But it was *you* who first gave me the idea of coming here,' Shelly protested.

'Me?' David's fork had stopped half-way to his mouth. 'How?' he demanded.

She sighed. 'Let's get one thing straight. You remember you spoke about——' the phrase stuck in her throat '—about taking Gail to court?'

'Clearly,' he rasped.

'You must admit the idea was a little...hot-headed?'

'Must I?'

'Yes,' she declared. Shelly experienced a moment of relief. Maybe he had not agreed with her statement, yet neither had he dissented. It represented some kind of progress. 'You know as well as I do that any case you instigated wouldn't stand a chance,' she continued.

His expression darkened. 'I assume this means you're giving notice that your sister intends to hang on to the pottery come hell or high water, and the family can go whistle for its twenty thousand pounds?'

'You could put it like that,' Shelly agreed, irritated by his use of 'the family' again. 'However, it'd also be fair to say that Mrs Wilkins is perfectly entitled to celebrate a relationship which is vastly important to her in whatever way she wishes—and that Gail is perfectly entitled to retain any gift she is given.' A mouthful of fish was eaten. 'But to explain why I'm here. If you remember, you spoke about me having skills I must be able to market? You were right, I do have skills, and——'

'Yeah?' he drawled.

The word was a slur, a taunt, an insult—yet, sorely tempted though she was, Shelly refused to react. 'I'm a physiotherapist,' she said, 'and I've come to Nevis to initiate an exercise programme which will ease Mrs Severney's arthritis. I don't know if you're aware of this, but I've been treating Mrs Wilkins——'

David's head jerked up. 'You're the girl she's written about in her letters to Jessica?' he demanded. 'The one who works miracles?'

'Not miracles,' she said, trying hard not to smile. He had heard about her work—good. Very good. In praising her, Beatrice had smoothed the ground, prepared the way. All she needed to do now was slide into place. 'I can claim, however, to have achieved a marked improvement in her health and I plan to do the same for Mrs Severney.'

'No, thanks.'

Shelly stared at him. He had refused? Turned her down flat?

'I beg your pardon?' she said, convinced she could not have heard right.

'I don't want you to go anywhere near Jessica.'

'And why not?' she asked indignantly.

'To combat her arthritis Beatrice has worn copper plates in her shoes, bought blue glass beads from Turkey, consumed vast quantities of chlorophyll. You name a treatment, she's fallen under its spell. So if you think——'

'No,' Shelly cut in. 'If *you* think my exercises are just the latest fad and ineffectual——'

'They come under the heading of alternative medicine, don't they?' he demanded.

'Under the blanket term, yes; but what does that matter? Mrs Wilkins is home from hospital, so why don't you call and ask if she feels the improvement was genuine, and whether or not it's been sustained.'

'I thought we'd agreed Beatrice is a crackpot?'

'No, we hadn't,' she disputed hotly, 'and even if her taste in art is odd, it doesn't render her incapable of knowing when her own health has taken a distinct turn for the better!'

He said nothing, and when he returned to his meal she resumed hers. The fish was full of flavour, the sauce piquant, the vegetables garden-fresh—yet everything tasted like cardboard. Shelly felt uncertain, uncomfortable, unhappy. A degree of willingness on David Llewellyn's part was vital, so had she twisted arms at the surgery, had she spent her hard-earned savings, had Gail sold the jewellery, all for nothing? What was she supposed to do—dismiss the rationale responsible for her journey as so much fanciful thinking?

'I take it Jessica's agreed to this treatment?' he enquired, as he helped himself to some more wine.

'I'd hardly be here otherwise.'

'She's never said anything to me about it.'

Shelly was not surprised. Reveal your plans, hopes, dreams to David Llewellyn, and he would swat them like flies.

'No doubt Jessica's paying handsomely for your services,' he observed, as they finished eating. 'Tell me, has the figure already been decided, or do you work on a *pro rata* basis and hit her with a four-digit sum at the end of your stay?'

Shelly resisted hitting *him*—just. 'I'm treating Mrs Severney for free,' she replied sweetly.

His mouthful of wine went down the wrong way. 'For—for free?' he spluttered.

'As Mrs Wilkins has helped Gail, so I would like to help Mrs Severney.'

He lacerated her with a look. 'How, by getting her to do arms-stretch, knees-bend, ra-ra-ra, then coating her with honey and dung and standing her in a cupboard to dry?'

'I'm not a quack!' she flashed.

David took another drink from his glass. It went down properly this time.

'You have diplomas?' he queried. 'Could I see them?'

Shelly knew she reddened, and was thankful for the gloom. 'Do you walk around with your pilot's licence in your hip pocket?' she shot back. 'No, you don't, and neither do I carry around my credentials. I accept that one school of thought believes in pumping arthritis sufferers full of chemicals day in and day out, but many people prefer to seek a natural form of relief. Have you never thought that all pain-killing drugs do is camouflage? And that anything you put into your body alters its balance in a way which the scientists can't always predict?' she demanded, her belief in her creed gathering momentum. 'Over the years there've been a series of drug disasters which——'

The justification stopped dead. The chef, a brawny young man in kitchen whites and tall hat, had been going the rounds of the tables and now he materialised beside them.

'Hi, Pieter.' All of a sudden David brimmed with an easy charm. 'How's tricks?'

'Not bad,' the new arrival grinned. 'Still looping the loop?'

'Only on Sundays.'

This proved to be the start of a jokey male repartee, for which Shelly gave thanks. She needed a respite from the cut and thrust, needed to calm down. Her aim in coming to Nevis had been to *please* David Llewellyn, not to act as sparring partner. But how could you possibly gladden the heart of a man like him?

'You look as if you made a detour into the ocean on your way up to dinner, *ya*?' the chef quipped, eyeing his still-damp shirt. 'Or did you come straight from the jacuzzi?'

Shelly received an ice-axe glance.

'Thanks to Miss Havers, I suffered a mishap.'

'You're Miss Havers?' the young man exclaimed, in what she had identified as a Dutch accent. He wrapped a huge paw around her fingers and jerked her hand up and down. 'Mrs Severney has told me how unselfishly you toil, how you dedicate yourself to improving the quality of life for others. I applaud your humanity.'

'Thank you,' she said, and could not resist shooting David a triumphant glance. Never mind if the chef had made her sound embarrassingly next in line for a sainthood, at least he was positive. 'And, please, call me Shelly,' she appealed, gratitude for his compliments lifting her smile into the de luxe category.

'Shelly,' he beamed. 'Enjoying your meal?'

'Excellent.'

'Dessert's on its way. Tonight's speciality is banana soufflé. I guarantee it'll melt in your mouth.'

'Looks good,' she assured him, as the waitress appeared on cue to spoon out helpings from a silver tureen.

'You can give me your verdict in the lounge when you have coffee,' the Dutchman said, with a wink. 'I must be off and talk to our other guests. *Ciao.*'

'Ciao,' she smiled.

'How much would it take to get you to leave Nevis?' David demanded as the chef walked away. 'If I flew you over to Antigua early tomorrow, you could connect with the London flight.'

'Leave? Leave tomorrow?' Shelly repeated, in astonishment. 'But I've only just arrived!'

He scowled back over his shoulder. 'Could you raise your voice a couple more octaves? I don't think the guy in the far corner heard.'

'You expect me to reply to a suggestion like that in a whisper?' she hissed.

'I expect you to reply with a quiet affirmative.'

'Then you're out of luck!'

'A couple of days in a hotel, and a hundred dollars on top. How's that?'

'Would you stop trying to buy me off?'

'Would you keep your voice down?'

'Can't you see that I'm here to help Mrs Severney?' Shelly demanded. She took a spoonful of the soufflé. 'This is delicious.'

For a full minute he studied her from across the table, then he sighed and also turned his attention to the dessert.

'What are these exercises of yours supposed to do?' David enquired after a while.

'Reduce pain and increase flexibility. People with arthritis tend to shy away from activity and grow stiff, which in turn worsens the illness. A vicious circle is set up, one I break up by using a combination of calisthenics and yoga positions. Naturally, the results vary from person to person, but I can guarantee that in two months' time Mrs Severney will be feeling much better.'

He crumpled his napkin. 'Yeah?'

'Yes. I realise your views on medicine are ultra-conservative,' Shelly went on, eager to take advantage of what she hoped might be a softening in his attitude, 'and I agree that that's your prerogative, but I shan't be asking Mrs Severney to do anything hazardous, nor will I raise false hopes. Mrs Wilkins will verify everything,' she appealed, when he frowned.

'Whether or not she's a crackpot, Beatrice *is* a pushover,' David retorted. 'Give her a smile and she'll say—and do,' he added pungently, 'whatever it is you——'

As a possessive and scarlet-taloned hand clamped down on his shoulder, he froze. The redhead had sashayed over.

'I've arranged our coffee, Davie,' she told him, then glanced at Shelly. 'Care to join us?' she enquired unenthusiastically.

'No, thanks.' That her companion should have been claimed by a woman who looked a good fifteen years older was intriguing—particularly when the hardening of his jaw indicated he was far from pleased—but she had no intention of making up a threesome. 'If you'll excuse me, I'll go and see how Mr and Mrs Shepherd are settling in,' she said, and sped off.

In the 'instant pals' style of holidaymakers, the couple welcomed her, and suggested she join them in the corner of the lounge. Their chatter of the Labrador pup they had left back home, of how neither of them had flown so far before, of the walks they planned to take, made a soothing contrast to the previous highly charged dialogue. Shelly knew she should relax. She recognised the ideal opportunity to banish David Llewellyn from her mind. Yet, as the Shepherds gossiped on, her gaze deviated. She did not want to look at him, but her eyes were compelled—as they would have been to a scene of an accident. There were glimpses of him being courted by the redhead, cracking a joke with Wellington, talking to some of the other guests. From time to time he grinned, his full mouth tipping down to the left in a most attractive way. Why couldn't he grin at her like that? she wondered. Abruptly David raised his head and his blue eyes slammed into hers.

'You appear to have an admirer,' chuckled Mr Shepherd, as she flushed and snatched her gaze away.

She shook her head. 'Never.'

Mr Shepherd might not recognise a bruiser of a look when he saw one, but she could. The softening she thought she had detected earlier lay exposed as a vain hope.

'Don't be modest,' Mr Shepherd laughed. 'You've made a conquest, and here he comes.'

Shelly's tumbled composure was swiftly reassembled. If David had strapped on the gloves again, so be it. It was not her choice to enter the ring, and he threw a mean fist, but . . . She would not be pulverised into submission, would not be ousted, would not be pole-axed. She had come with the best intentions and, in the course of time, surely he must recognise she was one of the good guys and not the bad? But when she looked up it was to find Pieter striding along the room, his boyish face split into a smile. In red checked shirt and jeans, he looked very much off-duty and keen to socialise.

'Hello,' she said, relief sparkling in her welcome.

'Hi, there.' He greeted the Shepherds and sat down beside her. 'You enjoyed the soufflé?' he asked.

'The best ever,' she vowed.

'I wish mine turned out like yours,' lamented Mrs Shepherd, a birdlike woman with a tight perm and glasses. 'How do you get such a frothy texture?'

Pieter explained—at length and in impressive detail. Ingredients were listed and the method expounded until Mrs Shepherd's eyes began to glaze and several yawns were secreted behind her hand.

'Time we toddled off to bed,' she declared, the moment the young man had finished. Roping her husband with a look, she lifted him out of his seat to the door, where they collected torches and a golf brolly. 'Goodnight.'

Undeterred by their departure, Pieter moved on to other desserts. Shelly listened politely to one recipe after another until, once again, the tall, dark-haired man beside the bar proved annoyingly magnetic.

'David was saying he stays at the Great House to suit the Hawk-Air flights,' she inserted, as the Dutchman paused for breath. 'How often is that?'

To have arrived with such a cock-eyed grasp of the facts was a mistake. Now she intended to learn as much as possible, for the more hard data she had to hand, the better she could deflect whatever right-hooks were destined to be thrown her way next.

'He reckons his time's split roughly forty per cent on Antigua, forty per cent here, and the remainder on other assorted islands,' Pieter replied.

Shelly pulled a face. The percentage on Nevis was higher than she would have preferred, but at least he would not be continually around.

'A disjointed life-style,' she commented.

'It'd have me climbing the wall,' the young man agreed, 'but David goes wherever the work takes him. He never complains. If you ask how he stands it, he says the creation of an airline, or anything worthwhile, demands personal sacrifices. He's the kind of guy who, when he commits himself to an idea, commits himself in total. There are no half measures.'

'So I've noticed,' Shelly remarked drily. 'Moving around all the time must play havoc with his relationships,' she said, fishing for more.

Beatrice had given the impression her nephew was a bachelor, and he did not *seem* married, but if she had misjudged his location by a continent and an ocean, what chance had mere marital status?

'There are no relationships.' Pieter glanced along to where the redhead had corralled David again. 'Pearl tells me there's something about a man fighting the elements which is very, very sexy, and it's true that when they discover David's a pilot most women go starry-eyed. But he isn't interested.'

'Not at all?'

'The daughter of the guy who runs Creole Beach worked hard to start up a friendship, and they did go riding a few times, but the interest was all on her side. David wasn't taking, or giving. In my opinion she's well out of it. Don't quote me, and particularly don't say anything to Mrs Severney, because she thinks the world of him,' the young man cautioned, lowering his voice, 'but David has a ruthless streak. A couple of years ago he went off to Scotland and arrived back with a girl who'd been a stewardess with the airline he'd worked for there. I never saw her, but according to Wellington she was a real dazzler. Long brown hair down to her waist, a figure like——' He depicted an hour-glass. 'A wedding date was fixed, the guests invited, it was full-steam ahead to the altar, but at the last minute——' he clicked his fingers '—David wanted out.'

'Why?'

'Apparently Hawk-Air had more to offer him than matrimony. The tale goes that he'd been neglecting his fiancée for a fair time in the run-up to the ceremony, so I guess when he realised his highs came from business and not her, he decided he'd do better to cut loose. Ditching her was pretty cold-blooded when you consider that the girl had given up her job, left her family and her friends, in order to come out here and be his bride.' Pieter shrugged hefty shoulders. 'On the rebound she went and married a Frenchman who owns one of the premier holiday clubs on Antigua. It's a fantastic place, with a marina, golf course, casino. All the in-crowd holiday there,' he explained. 'Anyhow, the marriage was a failure from day one and now they're in the process of getting divorced.' He smoothed a hand over his fair, curly hair. 'How about me driving you around Nevis and showing you the sights? I could take you tomorrow?' he suggested. 'Or the next day? Or the day after that?'

Shelly smiled. 'Sorry, but I can't commit myself to anything until I've spoken to Mrs Severney.'

'The moment you're available, even if it's only for an afternoon, tell me. We'll go to Pinney's Beach first. Then, when you have a full day free, we shall visit——'

'I'd prefer to leave plans for later,' she said, surprised to find Pieter so much in earnest. This was only her first evening, and she bucked against being pressurised. Shelly rose and walked across to a brass-edged military-style table filled with enamelled snuff boxes. 'Aren't they beautiful?' she said, as the young man joined her. A silver galleon was marvelled at next, then a collection of tiny tea-bowls and saucers caught her eye. 'These are from the Nanking Cargo,' she said, with pleasure.

'Nanking?'

'You must have heard about it. A sailing ship called the Geldermalsen sank in the South China Sea in 1752, and when the porcelain was salvaged more than two hundred years later the divers found it intact.' She ran reverent fingers over a blue-and white-patterned saucer. 'This is the Batavian Bamboo and Peony design.'

'Quite the expert,' scythed a voice, and she swivelled to find David stood close behind her. 'Can you tell me their value?'

Shelly shook her head. 'I know they're collectors' items and expensive, but I couldn't give a price. Nanking is the only porcelain I can recognise,' she said, thrown on to the defensive because he was frowning as though he had caught her in the act of palming a saucer or two. 'I saw a television documentary about the cargo being raised, and Gail's also spoken about it. Being a potter, she finds the story of great interest.'

'At a guess I'd say you handsome gentlemen are the same height,' someone giggled. It was the redhead, arriving to grab both of them by an arm and sway between, posing and simpering. She grinned up at David. 'Six foot two and a half in your socks?'

'Something like that,' he dismissed.

'And you, Pieter?'

'Six three, Pearl, but thanks to my sampling in the kitchen I'm a good deal heavier than David,' he said, and mock-thumped him in the ribs.

'How do you manage to keep in such good shape, Davie?' Pearl enquired, painted eyes slurping from his head down to his toes.

'I worry.'

His admirer changed course. 'Your aunt was telling me how your great-grandfather came out here as a missionary. I was *fascinated*.'

'You must have been,' he grated.

Shelly, too, had been intrigued when Beatrice had spoken about the Welshman who had arrived to build a chapel in the Caribbean so many years ago. She would have liked to know more but, unlike the redhead, had recognised that David was in no mood for questions.

'Where is Mrs Severney this evening?' Pearl enquired, continuing to cling.

'At a hoteliers' meeting,' Pieter informed her. 'It cropped up suddenly, something to do with finalising a joint advertising campaign. That's why she wasn't here to greet you,' he told Shelly. 'She was very disappointed.'

'I believe you were born in Antigua, Davie,' the woman said, wresting the conversation back into her possession.

'I was.'

'And your parents live there now?'

'They do.'

'But you were educated in the States and you've worked for European airlines? You're quite the international man, Davie,' she gushed.

His blue eyes burned with impatience. 'It's *David*.' He stepped back, breaking her hold. 'Like me to deliver you to your cottage?' he asked Shelly.

'Oh, thanks,' she said, surprised by his consideration.

'It's all right, I'll walk her over,' Pieter announced, as though he possessed seigneurial rights.

'We're next door to each other,' David explained, his tone hinting that whoever had allocated the accommodation must have taken leave of their senses, 'so I'm heading that way anyway.'

As Pieter shrugged and Pearl sulked in the background, Shelly pulled on her mackintosh and joined him beneath the large umbrella. Any hopes that the weather might have eased were dashed in seconds. The wind still howled through the trees. The rain flung itself around. The darkness was like a black hole. Plodding beside him, she was forced to admit to a certain gratitude. David Llewellyn's self-sufficiency made it impossible to imagine anyone or anything daring to interrupt their journey. With him, she felt safe.

'It's good to know there's someone in the cottage beside me,' Shelly said, his sturdiness drawing out the confession.

He cast her a glance. 'Being there alone disturbs you?'

'It wouldn't do normally, it's just that in this kind of weather——' The heavens above them rumbled. 'Oh, no!'

'Something's the matter?'

'I don't like thunder.' Fearfully she peered up at the sky. 'Or lightning.'

'Would it help any if you held on?'

'Sorry?'

He raised his arm. 'It's going spare.'

'Er—thank you,' Shelly muttered, confused to find him offering help.

As she established a grip on his wrist, she felt a rough smattering of hair beneath her fingertips. The link comforted, and yet at the same time disturbed.

Although his offer ranked as no more than common courtesy, *touching* him generated a sharp awareness of her escort as a physically attractive male.

'Pearl appears to be rather taken with you,' she said, finding a sudden need to talk.

David gave a tortured groan. 'Like Jessica, I dine with the guests whenever I'm here,' he explained, 'and although I've spent numerous lively meals in the company of engaging people, there've also been occasions when I've needed to fight off unattached females. I happened to sit across from our desperate divorcée the other night and, for some reason, she decided irrevocable karma was responsible.'

Shelly laughed. 'You should be flattered.'

'If Pearl had her way, I'd be *flattened*,' he replied, and shuddered. 'Be they eighteen or eighty, all the single women who visit the Caribbean seem to come with one aim in mind—to grab themselves a romance.'

'Not me,' she said pertly.

They had reached her door.

'No, not you,' David agreed. As he surveyed her in the torchlight, his gaze became very penetrating, very intense. 'Why don't you reconsider my offer and let me fly you out in the morning?' he asked.

Shelly snatched her hand from his wrist. The intimacy of the last few minutes had gone a long way to cancelling the image of him as the get-the-hell-out-of-here heavyweight, but that was what he was! Now she knew why he had offered to walk her over. It had had nothing to do with consideration, and everything to do with expediency.

'Why don't you reconsider the advantages of my treating your aunt?' she retaliated, then she sighed. 'There'd be no harm in your *thinking* about it.'

He scuffed the toe of his shoe across the wet grass. 'I guess not.'

'Then please do.' Her key was inserted and the door opened. 'Tomorrow I shall buy myself a torch and an umbrella, and——'

'You needn't bother,' David interrupted. 'Look inside the bedroom cupboard and you'll find one of each provided for your personal use.'

She swung to him. 'I've had my own all along?'

'Standard equipment.'

'You could have told me!'

He heaved a noisy sigh. 'What do you imagine I intended to do when I followed you earlier?'

'But if you'd said, I would have been able to have gone back and collected them,' Shelly retorted, unreasonably vexed to discover she had been relying on his company, the umbrella, his wrist, for no reason at all. 'Then I could have walked over to the hotel on my own and returned on my own.'

'You prefer to be independent?'

'I do.' She stepped over the threshold. 'Thanks for the helping hand, but I shan't be needing your services again.'

'You're sure?'

Her chin took on a regal tilt. 'I am.'

'In that case, sweetface,' David said, striding towards his own door, 'you may be certain my services won't be offered!'

CHAPTER FOUR

To Shelly's relief, the storm blew itself out overnight and she awoke next morning to a tranquil, washed-clean world, vivid with colour. When she walked to the Great House it was across verdant, velvety lawns, beneath a sky of china-blue. Green-yellow palm fronds rustled in the warm breeze, and in the distance white-topped waves rippled a sea of aqua. This was the Caribbean of the travel posters. The Caribbean of sunshine and song and laughter. The Caribbean where all you met were friendly, smiling faces. All? She crossed her fingers, and offered up a fervent entreaty that yesterday's combative reception in no way presaged the one arranged for today. When telephoned, Beatrice's sister had expressed an acute desire for assistance, but—despite his agreement to reconsider—it was always possible David had spoken to her this morning and soured everything.

Mrs Severney, a smiling, grey-haired lady dressed in a navy linen two-piece and pearls, appeared as Shelly was finishing breakfast. Her greeting was warm and, as questions were asked regarding both Beatrice's and her own welfare, Shelly's tension slackened. The nephew—whose absence in the dining-room had been a distinct aid to the digestion—might possess high-visibility doubts, but the aunt was receptive and agreeable. After giving her name as Jessica and insisting it must be used, the old lady suggested they go across to her home.

'We won't be disturbed here,' she said, leading the way towards a tiny bleached-brick cottage on one side of the Great House. 'Despite my sister writing page after page, I have only a sketchy idea of what it is you actually do,' Jessica confessed, when they were settled on a patio shaded by purple bougainvillaea and trellised vines. 'Beatrice tends to skip over specifics.'

And how! Shelly thought wryly, and began to explain about her exercises. 'I'm here to develop a programme suited to your particular needs,' she said, 'plus I'd like to discuss your diet and life-style, and maybe suggest changes.'

'Such as?'

'You should avoid doing one activity for any length of time, so I'd advise against long hours at a desk.' She adjusted the collar of her beige cotton jumpsuit. 'But I expect your doctor's warned you about that already?'

'I haven't spoken to him,' Jessica confessed. 'Unless something's drastically wrong, he isn't interested.'

'You must make an immediate appointment,' Shelly said sternly. 'Although I'm able to assess the extent and nature of your condition up to a point, his diagnosis is essential.'

'You sound like David, my nephew. He's been on at me for months to consult someone. He says the longer my arthritis goes unattended, the worse it'll get.'

'He's right.'

'But now you're here, thank goodness.' Jessica fingered her pearls. 'I imagine you must have come across David last night?'

'We dined together.'

The disclosure caused a widening of grey eyes and the necklace became worry beads.

'I haven't seen him this morning—a call came through from a landowner who wanted stock transported not one minute later than immediately, so he was gone at dawn—but I trust he wasn't . . . impolite? David does have a tendency to be over-protective at times, to be somewhat cautious-minded, but that's because——' Jessica hesitated, frowning. 'Well, things have happened in the past.'

Shelly nodded. 'I know.'

'He told you?' the older woman asked, looking at her in blank-faced astonishment.

'He explained how the sculptor and his wife——'

'Oh—oh, yes.' Jessica tucked a wisp of grey into the smooth bun which sat at the nape of her neck. 'David did behave himself?' she persisted. 'The reason I ask is because when I suggested coming to see you in Wales, he didn't agree. To be frank, he was dead set against it. He felt Beatrice was just under the *illusion* you were helping her. Please don't be offended, my dear. As a girl, my sister leant towards the—um—offbeat, you see, and lately she's had the misfortune to meet a scoundrel or two. So—um you can't blame David for thinking that maybe you were—um——'

Mrs Severney had become pink and flustered.

'He was the perfect gentleman,' Shelly declared, not having the heart to denounce him as the sceptic and bigot he had shown himself to be. 'Now, shall we get back to your arthritis?'

After an exchange of information, she tested her patient's mobility and took her through a trial session of exercises. In the belief that there was no greater encouragement for reluctant limbs than another body working out alongside, Shelly always joined her patients, and together they went through a series of slow movements designed to stretch and elongate.

'The sessions will increase each day until they last for thirty minutes,' she explained, as they finished. 'It'll be a while before you notice a diminishing of the pain, but after a week you should begin to feel more elastic.'

'You don't know how much I appreciate your taking the time and trouble to come out here,' Jessica smiled. She delved deep into her handbag and produced a cheque-book. 'I must reimburse you for your air ticket.'

An emphatic shake of Shelly's head sent the strands which varied from honey-blonde to palest gold swinging across her shoulders. 'When I told you on the phone that my services were free, I meant completely. I'm funding my travel, accommodation and all other expenses.'

'No. I'm sorry, my dear, but——'

'Mrs Wilkins has been very good to my sister,' Shelly said, treading carefully because she had no idea whether or not Jessica knew about the pottery, 'and Gail and I want to do something in return.'

Reluctantly, the cheque-book was put away. 'We'll forget about the ticket, but if you imagine I'd allow you to pay to stay at my hotel—I won't hear of it.'

Shelly recalled David's stinging condemnation of the sculptor and his wife. Whatever happened, he must not be able to accuse *her* of freeloading.

'Please, financing myself is important,' she appealed.

'Not allowed. If you insist, then the exercise sessions are off.' Behind the gentle smile lurked a stubborn streak. 'I mean it.'

Shelly undertook some fast thinking.

'I'll stay at the Great House for nothing—and thank you very much indeed—but only on one condition,' she bargained. 'That my services are extended to your friends, associates, guests, anyone who can benefit from exercise and/or massage; no matter whether they suffer from arthritis or not.'

'That's extremely generous,' Jessica smiled.

'Would you be agreeable to me pinning a notice up in the hotel, advising that a physiotherapist is ready, willing and able?' she asked, saying goodbye to the concept of having mostly a holiday.

From now on work was not just her first priority, it must be the only one. Though for her work and pleasure were often the same.

'Go ahead.'

'Can you think of anyone who'll be interested?' Shelly enquired eagerly.

The older woman laughed at her enthusiasm.

'I'm sure I'll be able to come up with several names, given the chance. I know Vanilla Brandy, for one, would love to see you. She's always complaining about problems with her "old bones". Vanilla's a local lady who lives on the outskirts of Charlestown. I could ring her.'

'Good. If you can arrange a time, I'll order myself a taxi and——'

'Do you drive? The hotel runs a spare moke,' Jessica said, when she nodded. 'Please use it.'

'Thanks. I'd be grateful if you could circulate news of my presence here as quickly and as widely as possible. I don't want to work part-time, I want to work all day,' Shelly declared. 'So if you can't round up enough patients you may well find me alongside Pieter in the kitchen, elbow deep in the washing-up!'

'I'll see what I can do,' Jessica chuckled. 'Speaking of Pieter, when you're out on the road and you suspect he may be, too, do keep on the alert. He's tame enough with a wooden spoon in his hand, but put him behind a steering wheel and he becomes Guy the Gorilla. The island has only one main road and it's a narrow, winding affair, but he treats it like a racetrack. Pieter's had so many near-misses, everyone runs for cover the minute they hear he's on the loose.'

She grimaced. 'He suggested we take a drive together.'

'If you get into a vehicle with that young man, I warn you you'll come back with hair as grey as mine—so make an excuse. Tell him you'd rather fly a kite, catch butterflies, anything.' Jessica's warning might be offered lightly, but it was genuine. 'It'll take me a day or two to contact my friends and broadcast news of your offer so, for now, I insist you relax. Trot down to the beach and work on a tan. Everyone's allowed to recover from jet lag. Even eager beavers!'

Secretly relieved to have time in which to come down to earth and find her bearings, Shelly stepped leisurely through the day. After exploring the Severney acres, which included an ancient sugar mill and a stream, she changed into her bikini and wandered down to the seashore. She was stretched out on a towel when the Shepherds passed by. 'Come and have lunch,' they entreated, so she tied on a poppy-patterned sarong and joined them. Other guests had already congregated in the beach bar, which comprised a few wooden tables shaded with banana-leaf roofs, and the mood was casual. Everyone spoke to everyone else. Everyone joked. Everyone was light-hearted.

Mid-afternoon, Shelly returned to her cottage. Pearl might strip to a squirm-inducing minimum and endlessly barbecue herself, but she was wary of too much sun. Also, yesterday's journey had caught up with her and she felt sleepy.

Once again she awoke in the dark, but this time the evening was still and balmy, so clear you could count the stars which twinkled high in the black sky. Gratifyingly, the power functioned, too. After showering she changed into a silky sapphire shirt with padded shoulders, zipped on black trousers, then headed towards the Great House in good time for dinner. As she walked, Shelly kept her chin well up, her backbone straight. There had been no signs of life next door, but if David was in residence she had no intention of him being able to look out of his window and notice another 'shadow flitting'. This time he would see a confident and capable young woman with a determined stride.

In the event her performance went unnoticed, because this evening turned out to be one of the times when he rested his head elsewhere.

'My nephew's in Barbados,' Jessica explained, in response to Pearl's queries. 'But I can't say for how long.'

'I hope he comes back soon,' his admirer whined. 'I miss his blue eyes. *Cobalt*-blue.'

Over the next couple of days, while the redhead chatted up every stray man she could find, and even those with wives in tow, Shelly set about organising herself. When approached, a number of Jessica's contemporaries owned up to possessing an ache or a pain somewhere, and the novelty of a physiotherapist visiting them in their own homes was too much to resist. A schedule was planned, one which, although it included fallow periods, had her off to a good start. Shelly was satisfied. Experience said

Jessica's friends would tell their friends, and word of mouth would soon have her fully occupied.

When David returned, walking into the bar late on the fourth evening, Pearl pounced.

'There's something so attractive about a man in uniform,' she trilled, her gaze devouring his white short-sleeved shirt with its black and gold epaulettes, his black trousers, the cap in his hand. 'Where have you been? What have you been doing? Why the delay?'

His prised-out replies failed to reach the table where Shelly was sitting with Pieter, but the redhead's rinky-dink exclamations dispersed the news that he had spent the last few days ricocheting from one problem to another.

'We take a tour around the island tomorrow, *ya*?' the young Dutchman suggested, as he drank the dregs of his lager. 'We visit the silk cotton tree where Nelson and Fanny Nisbet plighted their troth, motor on to the museum and inspect the Admiral's memorabilia, and later——'

'I'm busy,' Shelly apologised, awarding Pieter top marks for tenacity. Each evening he had joined her after dinner and pushed to fix a date for a drive—and each evening she had wriggled out of it.

'We go Saturday,' he stated.

'As the weather's like it is, I'd prefer to wait and see,' she said, firmly stonewalling.

After three placid sunny days, the wind had risen and at dusk there had been a cloudburst. Shelly had rushed to the Great House with umbrella held aloft, and still the rain splashed down. What did she do—return to her cottage now, or wait a few minutes on the off chance that it might lessen? In the midst of deciding, Shelly's skin prickled. She was under surveillance, and the scrutineer, she knew, was David. Throughout Pearl's questioning his eyes had repeatedly travelled to her, and each time his gaze had been sombre. Her heart plummeted. What could this continual watchfulness mean except that, after giving due consideration to her treatment of Jessica, he had arrived back where he started—determined to veto? She sighed. Tomorrow she would be prepared to stride from her corner and do battle, but not at this time of night.

'I must go,' she announced.

Pieter leapt to his feet. 'I'll walk you over.'

'Thanks, but there's no point you tramping all that way in the rain.'

As he occupied a bedsit on the ground floor of the Great House itself, declining his offer made sense. Yet what bothered Shelly was not so much him getting wet, but the conviction that if Pieter took her back to the cottage he would expect a goodnight kiss—or more. Probably more, for, with a speed which stunned and no encouragement at all, he had begun working towards a liaison. He sat a bit too close—until she moved away. His hand reached for hers—though she made sure it never hit target.

'I don't mind,' he assured her.

'I do.'

She collected her mackintosh, flung him a smile, and shot out into the darkness. On flying feet, Shelly headed home. By now, she had covered the distance so often that her journey had become commonplace. No longer did she see dreadlocks shaking above, no longer did she fear attack from an alien source. Even so, it was good to reach her cottage and get into the dry. After cleaning her teeth and pulling on the midnight-blue camisole top and briefs she wore for bed, she lay down. Tomorrow she had four appointments with Jessica's friends, plus a woman who was staying at the hotel had shown an interest. Should she suggest they get together in the late afternoon, she wondered, as she switched off the light, or did that seem too pushy? She closed her eyes. Perhaps she would do better to wait, and let the woman come to her? Perhaps——

Crash! Thwack! Boom! An earsplitting noise shot Shelly upright. Had a thunderbolt fallen? Was this an earthquake? Maybe the roof had caved in? Heart at the gallop, her head throbbing with the suddenness of it all, she blinked into the darkness. Fearing the worst but not having the least idea what the worst could be, she switched on the bedside-lamp. To left and to right her eyes swivelled, then up and down. Nothing. The room looked as it always did. The sounds were normal, too. Just the thrum of raindrops and the swirl of the wind. What had happened?

In jerking awake, her impression had been of a vibrating boom overhead, but maybe the tiny sitting-room at the front of the cottage was the epicentre? The strap of her camisole had become dishevelled in her fright, and Shelly hooked it back on to her shoulder. Ignorance was not bliss. She could not spend the remainder of the night awake and wondering. Whether a door ripped off its hinges or a collapsed ceiling awaited, she must investigate. Swinging her feet to the floor, she padded across the tiles. Tentatively, she poked out her head.

The taut insect netting screen which comprised the front wall of the sitting-room was speckled with rain, and outside the moon cast a gloom of shadows. Shelly frowned. Nothing here looked amiss, either. Intent on a closer inspection, she had taken one stride forward when a sound, like a stiletto slashing through heavy silk, tore across the night. A flare of dazzling white lit the room, transforming black into arc-light day. She gave a soundless sob. It was lightning, demonic and ruthless in its intensity. Seconds later, thunder roared in a crack which was so close, so powerful, that the cottage shook.

Despite the heat—a clinging, cloying heat which ground relentless fingers against her temples—Shelly shivered violently. What defence did a fragile speck of humanity have against this fury, this indiscriminate electricity, this atmospheric brawl? Ready to rush back to bed and bury her head under the pillow, a movement outside stopped her. It was David emerging from his side of the cottage. Fully dressed, he must have recently returned from the Great House.

'Everything OK?' he called.

'Perfect,' she claimed, recalling her haughty insistence that she would not be requiring his services again. Lightning streaked the sky. 'No, it's not,' she yelped, and rushed to open the door.

'It was a coconut,' he said, coming in. He ruffled his hair to shake off the rain. 'The crash just now,' David explained, when she gazed at him in bewilderment, 'was a coconut falling on the roof. It doesn't happen too often, but when it does, they don't come quietly. What's the damage?'

Vaguely she looked around. 'I—I don't think there is any.'

'He frowned. 'Then why tell me——'

Thunder cracked. Rooted to the spot one instant, Shelly leapt towards him the next. Even sparring partners had their uses, and this one stood tall and unafraid. In reflex his arms came round and for a moment he held her, then he jerked back.

'Don't play those tricks on me,' David grated, shoving his hands into his trouser pockets and glowering.

Mesmerised by the storm, Shelly switched her eyes from the scene outside, to him, and returned to the night again.

'What tricks?'

'Getting me in here under false pretences, then throwing yourself at me when you're half naked.'

A neon zigzag split the sky. She blenched. Last time the lightning and thunder had been virtually simultaneous. Now she detected an eerie gap.

'I'm not half naked!' she muttered, waiting, wondering, knowing the thunder must come—but when, when, oh, lord, when?

'No?'

Following his gaze, Shelly saw to her dismay that her strap had slipped again to reveal the high curve of a creamy breast. Only the jut of her nipple had stopped the silk from falling completely.

'I didn't get you in under false pretences,' she substituted, hastily tugging the camisole back into place.

'I can imagine Pearl resorting to this kind of tactic,' David scoffed, 'but it surprises me that you can't come up with something more original.'

'You think I want to—seduce you?' she spluttered, temporarily forgetting about what was happening outside. 'Huh, my imagination might step out of line occasionally, but yours has run amok!'

'So inviting me in with the declaration that the cottage has been damaged when it hasn't is legit?'

'Yes! Good grief, I might sleep alone, but I do so from choice. I'm not so frustrated I need to go around propositioning people!' Shelly exclaimed, her tone thick with disgust.

'You don't want to distract me, soften me up, get me on your side? Fine, fine, I've got it wrong,' he said tetchily, 'so you can stop looking at me as though I'm covered in open sores.'

Her strap had taken another walkabout, and she hooked it back on to her shoulder. 'I invited you in because I don't like storms, remember? But——' a mighty clap of thunder thrust her arms down by her sides, balled her hands into rigid fists '—but I realise now I'd do better seeking comfort from the god Thor, so I'd be grateful if you would go.'

'Tropical storms are more intense than the ones you'll be used to,' David pronounced, as though he was a meteorologist commencing a dissertation, 'but they're no reason to get uptight.'

'Some people detest spiders, others faint at the sight of a dentist; I happen to hate this type of weather, whether it occurs on the Equator or at the South Pole,' Shelly informed him, through gritted teeth. She quailed at a zip of lightning. 'Now, please go!'

'You're trembling.' He stretched out a hand and touched her arm. 'The cottages have lightning conductors. They're earthed. Nothing's going to happen.'

'I know,' she said, then gazed at him in horror as thunder pummelled the heavens again.

David cupped sturdy, long-fingered hands around her shoulders.

'Don't be upset,' he entreated, in a different, gentler voice. 'You're perfectly safe.'

'Y-yes,' she faltered, thinking she would be far safer under the bed or hidden in a cupboard—any place where she could stick her fingers in her ears and hum loudly, and block out sight and sound of the tempest.

'You are,' he insisted.

'I believe you. Or, at least, my head believes you, but——' Lightning jagged. Shelly swallowed hard. 'I wish the storm would move on.'

'It will.'

'When?'

Engulfed by a sudden and inescapable need to console, support and—yes, cherish, David drew her closer. His image of her as someone on the make had blurred. All he could see was a distraught and beautiful girl struggling to conquer a deep-seated fear. How could he resist her vulnerability? How could he ignore the expression in those luminous pools of eyes which pleaded 'help me'?

'Soon,' he murmured.

Shelly took a precarious stab at a smile. 'Promise?'

'I promise. Have you always been frightened?' he asked.

'Ever since I was five. That was when——'

'Hey,' David protested, as she flinched at a crash of thunder. He wrapped his arms around her. 'Hey, be brave.'

'I'm trying.'

'What happened?'

'I was playing in the garden,' she said, wondering how long she would need to sweat it out before the next spear of lightning. 'It was one of those hot, muggy, summer days when the sky turns leaden and the only thing which'll clear the air is a storm. When the rain started I went to the back door, but the handle was stiff and I couldn't open it.' Fleetingly, anxiously, she searched the night. 'I knocked, I shouted, I rushed round to the front of the house and banged on the door there, but my mother didn't hear me. By this time it was pouring down, so I ran to collect my dolls. I'd left them under some trees and they were dry, and it seemed like the best thing was to stay there, too.'

'Why didn't your mother come looking for you?' David asked. 'She must have seen the rain.'

''Fraid not. When the thunder began I was scared, and when the lightning began I started to cry.'

'Did you try to rouse your mother again?'

Shelly nodded. 'I ran and thumped on the doors a second time, but there was no reply.'

'What the hell was she doing?' David demanded.

Her eyes were level with the knot of his tie, and now she subjected it to an intense examination. Why had she started to tell him this? she wondered. Why? It could only have been because where she had expected abrasiveness, she had stumbled upon his solicitude. And because she had been too snarled up in the weather to think where talking about her mother might lead.

'She was asleep. I'd gone back to my dolls when suddenly the air crackled and there was an enormous, malicious roar,' Shelly continued, speaking quickly to head off any more questions. 'I looked round and saw a tree behind me glimmer with white blinding light, then explode. Flames ripped through it and in seconds burning branches were falling everywhere.'

'You could have been killed!' David exclaimed, his voice rough with protest.

'The force of the blast threw me off my feet and I really did see stars. The next thing I knew I was pounding my fists on the door and screaming. How I got there, I don't know.' A lump had formed in her throat, and she swallowed. Whenever she remembered the terrified little girl she had been, she became distressed. 'A neighbour heard and rushed to the rescue.'

'And through all this your mother never woke up?' he demanded.

'No. So now, whenever the air grows heavy, it feels like it's pressing me down, pressing me in. There's nothing else I can do, but run away and hide.'

'You haven't hidden tonight,' David said.

Shelly gave a tiny laugh, surprised to realise that, for once in her life, she had actually managed to stay put.

'They say there's a first time for everything.'

'Your mother must have been pretty shaken when she realised what had happened.'

'It was Dad who made the fuss,' she replied, not thinking. 'When he arrived home from work and learned what had happened, he was horrified.'

'Your mother wasn't?' David persisted.

'She regretted it, of course, but——' Shelly attempted an offhand smile '—she had other things on her mind. She was an actress,' she continued, when the intent blue of his gaze made it clear more details were expected. 'Her career dominated her life to the extent that everything else—a husband, kids—languished on the periphery.'

'Would I have heard of her?'

'No. She wasn't successful, not even mildly, that's what made her obsession so pointless. Before she was married she did appear in a West End play, but the role didn't lead to anything. You see, although my mother looked the part, she couldn't *act* the part. Any part.' Shelly sighed. 'The critics said so, the director of the play said so, that all she managed afterwards was the occasional walk-on role said so, but she refused to face up to the truth. She went for endless auditions, learned endless lines, but it was cloud-cuckoo land. At the time she and Dad were married she claimed she was "resting". She "rested" until Gail had been born, then decided that the world had been starved of her talents for long enough. She started going up to London for auditions, and when the acting jobs failed to materialise she blamed my father. She maintained that if he hadn't intruded at the peak of her career she'd have been a star. She insisted he'd cheated her and——' Shelly raised and lowered her shoulders. 'To cut a long story short, my parents were divorced when Gail was two.'

David frowned. 'And you were?'

'Six.'

'And afterwards, did your mother continue to believe success waited around the corner?'

'Now there wasn't a husband holding her back, all things were supposed to be possible! She was continually dumping Gail and me, and heading off for try-outs. We seemed to spend more time in the neighbours' houses than in our own,' she said ruefully. 'It would have been better if my father had kept us after they separated, but in those days a man obtaining custody of his children was rare. Dad tried, but my mother insisted we go with her.' Shelly grimaced. 'I suspect she felt that giving up two little girls wouldn't be too good for the image when she hit the big time. At first Dad watched over us, but then he remarried and had another family to consider.'

'Sounds as if you and your sister must have brought yourselves up,' David remarked.

'On the whole, we did. My mother died eighteen months ago, and I know this sounds lousy, but although Gail and I were sad, our main feeling was one of relief. You see, when she didn't get parts her reaction was to——' Abruptly Shelly realised she had brought herself to the brink of a painful indiscretion. 'She became depressed. After she died, Gail went through a low period, too,' she continued hastily. 'She felt life had dealt her a raw deal, that she'd always been neglected.'

'I'd say the two of you had.'

'Maybe, but Gail reckoned it was different for me because for years Gareth, my boyfriend, had been around,' she explained, 'whereas she had no one. It was when she was in the middle of feeling lost that she met Mrs Wilkins. The friendship surprised me because, like you, I felt they made a strange couple, then I realised they both had huge gaps in their lives. Your aunt needed a child to love. Gail was desperate for a mother. Beatrice has become a surrogate one—well, a surrogate grandmother. She's always supportive, always affectionate, always *interested*. You can't imagine how much happier Gail is now.'

Lightning forked the sky and Shelly jumped.

'It won't hurt you,' David said, holding her tight.

'You'd think that, knowing why storms affect me, I'd be able to rationalise my fear and take them in my stride,' she said, adopting a defiantly jaunty tone. 'Lightning isn't supposed to strike twice.'

He ran the back of his fingers along her cheek. 'Sweetface, after an experience like that anyone would be scared, and scarred.'

'Even you?'

David's mouth tipped down. 'I may have given you the impression I was raised in a cave by wolves, but I am human.'

'Human enough to make mistakes,' she rebuked, when another rumble of thunder sounded. 'You promised the storm would go.'

'It will.' His lips brushed her brow. 'Just wait.'

'For how long?'

'I can't tell you that,' he murmured. 'But for however long it takes, I'll be here.'

'Thanks.'

Their eyes met and clung. There was a long, still moment when Shelly heard a distant bell go *ting*. He bent his head, and tenderly his mouth touched her mouth. Her senses whirled. For a moment the caress hovered as a butterfly caress of reassurance, then another emotion gained control. The pressure of his lips increased, requesting a response. David was kissing her. After an initial moment of shock, she kissed him back. How could she do otherwise, when his skin smelled of sandalwood and rain, when the arms around her were strong, when the body fitted against hers was sending battalions of hormones rushing to remote places?

As his mouth opened against hers, Shelly raised herself on tiptoe and wound her arms around his neck. Stretched up and into him, she became aware of the heat of his chest, the rub of his cotton shirt against her skin. Her breast was naked. Once more the camisole had slid.

'Let me,' David said huskily, as she raised a hand to retrieve it.

He caught hold of the strap but then, with a low murmur of protest as though he could not help himself, his fingers stroked slowly down across her shoulder. Shelly's world tilted and spun. All she could focus on was the man who had awakened her every nerve, who had dilated her senses. Breath held, her skin tender and zinging, she longed—waited—yearned, for more intimate caresses. They did not happen. Instead, precipitately, unwaveringly, the dark blue silk was thrust back into place and all contact was broken. Lovemaking had screeched to a halt.

David squared his shoulders. 'Woody Allen was right,' he said.

Totally adrift, she gazed at him. What was she supposed to do—burst into wild laughter, or into tears? Or did she disintegrate into a thousand bewildered pieces?

'Right—right about what?' she asked.

'The unfathomableness of desire. You're a marvellous girl to look at, but hell, Shelly——' he plunged an unsteady hand through his hair '—we hardly know each other. That apart, an entanglement is the last thing I need, or want.' He frowned. 'And getting entangled with *you* is——'

'The thunder's stopped.'

The comment came straight off the top of her head. She did not have a clue about the thunder: whether it had ended or whether it had accummulated to a deafening crescendo. With her heart thumping so hard, she would not have heard cymbals crashing alongside. But she could not bear to be accused of being a phoney, a no-good, a trickster, by the man who, a second earlier, had been holding her close.

'Has it?' David took time to adjust his tie. 'According to Pearl——' he began gravely.

'Pearl?' she echoed, her thoughts uncoordinated and askew.

He nodded. 'She reckons that you and Pieter have been together every evening since you arrived.'

'So?' Shelly demanded, bristling. She might be having difficulty keeping track of his conversation, but she was in no mood to be maligned. 'Don't tell me you're frightened of *him* becoming entangled with me?'

'It's the other way around. I think you ought to know that Pieter's into revolving-door relationships.'

'Revolving door?'

'As one girl exits the next one enters. On a holiday island it's easy to arrange. The thing is, he goes overboard and swears undying devotion every time.'

'Is this why you were frowning at me earlier?' she asked.

David nodded. 'Pieter was obviously going through the old routine and——' he hesitated, as though wondering how best to phrase what came next '—I wouldn't want you to fall foul.'

'I can recognise a practised Romeo when I see one,' Shelly protested. Despite his so-recent rejection, it felt good to know he did not want her to get hurt. But to know he had accepted her presence on Nevis felt even better; for why warn her about Pieter unless she was to be around for a while? 'You promised to have another think about my treating Jessica,' she continued eagerly. 'Have you spoken to her?'

'Briefly.' His mouth tipped down. 'She claims she's already feeling better.'

'Some of my other people say that too, but, as I warned your aunt, it's wrong to be too bowled over too soon. Regrettably, bad days are part and parcel of arthritis, and a few steps of progress are often coupled with one stride back.'

'Your other people?' he queried.

'Jessica's introduced me to several of her friends who feel they can benefit from my attention. I've already visited two or three, and I'll be dropping in on the others over the next few days.'

'How much do you charge for house calls?' David demanded.

Shelly stared at him in dismay. The barriers had gone up, the aggression had crept in, once more he was on the attack.

'Not a thing,' she informed him crisply.

He seemed taken aback, though in his case taken aback was not that far. 'Do I look like a man who was born yesterday?'

'You look like a man with a nasty, suspicious mind!' she retorted, then heaved a sigh. 'I came with sufficient traveller's cheques to pay for my accommodation and meals because that was my intention, but Jessica said no. I argued. Still she refused. Treating her friends and her guests is my way of offsetting a debit with a credit.'

His jaw was massaged with slow fingers. 'You certainly seem determined to stay here,' he muttered.

'For two months, *yes*.' Shelly went to the door. 'Thanks for your company, it helped. However, the storm's moved away, it's late and I'm tired, so——'

'Two months,' he repeated, making it sound like a life sentence.

She bestowed a sugar-pie smile. 'Even a purveyor of hocus-pocus like me can't haul Jessica down the path of healing in thirty seconds flat.'

'I guess not.' David straightened. 'OK, two months you want, two months you've got.' As he reached the door, he paused and waggled an index finger. 'But if you're pulling any kind of a stunt, God help you!'

CHAPTER FIVE

Jessica interrupted her arm-circling and looked up at the sky. A small white plane, nose up in take-off mode, had appeared from the direction of the airfield. 'There he goes,' she said, shading her eyes to watch. 'I do hope he'll be all right.'

'Is something the matter?' Shelly asked.

'It's Pearl,' her companion chuckled, as the twin-engined craft levelled out and disappeared into the haze. 'This morning there were too many people to fit into one plane, so it was agreed that Ralph would fly over from Antigua and collect the first load, while David followed on with some cargo and whoever happened to be left. Wellington's just returned from the airfield with the news that there was one person surplus, and it happened to be the man-eater herself! How she wangled that they'd be alone together at last, I've no idea.'

Shelly laughed. 'You think she might lunge on him in mid-air?'

'There's a possibility. Pearl isn't the type who takes no for an answer or who gives up gracefully. Still, David's always on the alert, so I dare say he'll manage.'

Always on the alert. As Jessica returned to her exercises, Shelly sighed. Three weeks ago, she had known that David's waggling finger meant she remained on sufferance; yet she had firmly believed that, as time passed and no 'stunts' surfaced, his suspicions would recede. It was not so.

Whenever he had dined at the Great House, David had dined with her. This could have been interpreted as a gesture of friendship, even interest—Mr and Mrs Shepherd were convinced he was paying court—or, less flatteringly, a slick way of avoiding Pearl. But Shelly could recognise a stakeout. He might pretend to enjoy her company—and the conversation *did* flow and they *did* laugh together—yet whatever she had had to say had been noted, no doubt to be analysed and assessed. Now she had clambered up the learning curve high enough to know David trusted her so far, and no further. Shelly sighed again. Both his aunts had been deceived at one time or another, yet did their experiences justify him standing such ferocious guard? No. Never. He was guilty of gross overkill.

A loosening of knee joints brought the session to an end, and as her patient got to her feet she made a rapid assessment. Flexibility of movement, the smoothing of worry lines, new feelings of energy, all indicated that Jessica's well-being had been considerably enhanced. For the moment Shelly was content to wait, but the day would come when David would be required to acknowledge her expertise. That day promised to be sweet...yet would it make him any less chary?

'I'm so glad you persuaded me to lose that five pounds,' Jessica said, running a hand over her stomach. 'Being slimmer is a tremendous boost.'

'After I've showered I'm off to visit Mrs Brandy. I wonder if she's started on *her* diet?'

They exchanged a grin.

'I doubt it. Vanilla's full of good intentions, but she also believes in taking big bites out of life, and cakes, and enjoying herself.'

Driving along in the moke, Shelly had to admit that she, too, was taking a big bite out of life. Maybe she had supervised one exercise session, was heading for a second, and had two more lined up for this afternoon, but the sun was warm on her back, a light breeze tousled her hair, the sky above was blue. To her left the wooded slopes of Mount Nevis rose into a halo of cotton-wool mist. To her right spread coconut groves, and through them flashes of sparkling sea. The pink T-shirt and brief shorts she wore, an outfit which comprised her Caribbean working gear, imparted a holiday feeling. Certainly the people who greeted her—and the traffic was so sparse that everyone called hello—took it for granted she had nothing more on her mind then pleasing herself.

Avoiding a pot-hole and swerving past a foraging goat, she turned on to the main street of Charlestown, the island's port and capital. A conglomeration of old colonial houses and sun-baked squares, it had wound itself around her heart with its sleepy charm. On her first visit to Mrs Brandy, Shelly had lost her way, and in being helped to find it again seemed to have shaken hands with most of Charlestown's inhabitants. Today, when people called, she waved. Reaching her destination, she was required to wave again. Like so many Nevisian homes, Mrs Brandy's house had a first-floor veranda, and the lady was waiting with plump black arms resting on the rail.

After an exchange of greetings, the exercises began. Wide of smile and much wider of hip, Vanilla did her best with the side bends and leg raises, but when it came to the chair twist, she burst out laughing.

'Honey, there's no hope in heaven of me tucking in my chin and keeping my tummy flat!' she giggled. A side-table set with pitcher of iced guava juice and plate of coconut biscuits received a ravenous look. 'How's about we take a break?'

The break was taken, during which the rate at which Vanilla replenished lost calories was only exceeded by her apologies. Tomorrow she vowed she would diet. Tomorrow she would exercise. Tomorrow she planned to take a long walk.

'Before we start again,' she said, popping the last biscuit into her mouth and heading for the hall, 'let me show you what I've got for you.'

When she returned with arms spread wide, carrying a large, flat brown paper parcel, Shelly looked at her in dismay.

'Mrs Brandy, I really can't accept——' she started.

'This is just a little memento,' the black woman smiled. Vanilla was bending her head to wrestle with the too-tight string when brakes squealed outside on the street. A split-second later they heard a loud crash, a thump, the tinny wheeling of a hubcap. 'Mercy me!' she exclaimed, and hurried with Shelly on to the veranda.

Angled in the centre of crossroads up the hill they saw a cream Ford saloon, while jammed against an electricity pole was a pale blue mini-moke. The moke had taken the brunt of the impact: its bonnet was staved in, the windscreen shattered, and sections of bodywork had been scratched down to bare metal. The driver, a hefty young man with fair hair, hung out of one side.

'Oh, heavens, it's Pieter!' Shelly exclaimed.

'The roadhog Jessica's always warning everyone about?'

'The same.'

With Vanilla puffing in her wake, she rushed up to the junction. An Indian woman, looking shaken but unhurt, had climbed from the Ford, but the young Dutchman continued to lie half in and half out of the moke. His eyes were closed and he was moaning.

'Pieter, it's Shelly,' she said, kneeling down beside him.

His lids opened and he gazed at her, though it was difficult to detect any sign of recognition.

'I've banged my head,' he mumbled. His eyes slid away and returned. 'Thank you for coming, my darling, my dearest heart, my beloved. I knew you wouldn't let me down. *Ya*, I knew you cared.'

'He's delirious,' she told Vanilla, partly because it was true, but also to dispel any idea that they might be lovers. She eyed his awkward rag-doll sprawl. 'We'd better sit him up.'

As the two of them eased him back into the driving seat, Pieter winced.

'I might have broken my arm,' he slurred. 'And cracked a rib or two.'

'He doesn't look good,' Vanilla fretted, as he slumped back. Her fat cheeks wobbled. 'Not good at all.'

The young man's usually robust colour had drained, leaving him ashen. The arm he thought had been broken flopped by his side, while the other was scraped raw. A stain of blood, like a large medallion, matted the hair above one ear, and a thin stream trickled from a cut on his brow. But what worried Shelly the most was his confusion, his blinking, the difficulty he had in focusing.

'Can you ring for an ambulance?' she said to Vanilla.

'I could, but the hospital's less than a mile off. I figure it'd be quicker if you took him, honey.'

Shelly collected her moke, then acted as a careful crutch for Pieter while Vanilla heaved and steadied. When the young man had been transferred, she climbed in beside him.

'Left at the church, right at the jack-fruit tree, and straight on,' instructed the black woman. 'I'd come with you, only I'd better ring Jessica. She has a hotel full of guests, so she needs to know as soon as possible that she won't have a chef around to prepare dinner.'

Shelly drove off. With Pieter muttering and rolling his eyes, she could ill afford to lose her way, and when the small hospital turned out to be where Vanilla had said, she gave heartfelt thanks. The receptionist listened to her request for help, summoned porters, alerted a doctor, and in no time at all the young man was being lifted on to a stretcher.

In the lobby, he reached for her hand. 'You won't leave me here, Shelly?' he implored, in a moment of lucidity.

'I'll stay,' she assured him.

After the quick-quick admission, everything atrophied. Abandoned like a lost child, Shelly had nothing to do but wait. Thirty minutes, forty-five, sixty, dragged by. Why was Pieter's examination taking so long? What were his injuries? Was he all right? Repeated enquiries of the receptionist proved unproductive. Sorry, there was no news. She must be patient. Shelly leafed through the waiting-room's meagre supply of magazines, learned the view off by heart, paced endlessly to and fro.

The sound of footsteps brought her pacing to a standstill and she turned, anxiety throbbing like a pulse in her head.

'David!' she exclaimed, when the door burst open. 'Oh, David, am I glad to see you.'

Even though he was not a doctor bearing glad tidings, as a familiar face he was the next best thing. It was all she could do not to fling herself upon him and blubber her gratitude.

'What's happened?' he demanded, his blue eyes flying up and down her.

'Pieter collided with another car. I think he's broken his arm and——'

'Never mind him, what about you?'

Shelly looked nonplussed. 'I'm fine.'

He exhaled a breath. 'Thank God! When Wellington told me there'd been an accident, I imagined——' David's fears transformed themselves into anger, and he glared. 'You could have been seriously injured, if not killed, you know that? Jessica said she'd warned you about Pieter being a lousy driver. Why the hell didn't you take any notice?'

'I did!' she protested, astonished to find herself under attack. 'I wasn't with him.'

'You—you weren't?' he faltered. 'Then what's all that blood on your T-shirt?'

Shelly glanced down to find several dark stains. 'It's Pieter's. His head was bleeding and I must have got it on me when we shifted him from his moke to mine. I was at Mrs Brandy's when the crash happened further up the hill,' she explained. 'We went to help and I brought him to the hospital.' She frowned. 'How come Wellington told you? I know Vanilla was going to ring Jessica, but——'

'She did, and, in turn, Jessica passed on the news to Wellington. A little while later he happened to be collecting goods at the airfield and we met. I'd just flown in from Antigua. He gave me the story, though obviously his version was somewhat twisted,' David said drily. 'So—how is Pieter?'

'I wish I knew, but he was whisked away the moment we arrived, and since then——' palms up, her hands were spread wide '—nothing.'

'When did you arrive?'

Shelly consulted her watch. 'Over an hour ago.'

'And you've been sitting here ever since?' he said, flinging a look which roundly condemned her investigative powers.

'Not sitting. Interspersed with walking across this floor a million times, I've made frequent requests for a progress report. That I haven't received one is not——' a short, stocky, coloured man in a white coat had entered '—my fault,' she completed.

Much as Shelly welcomed the doctor's arrival, she found it irritating that he should have appeared promptly for David when she had been waiting on tenterhooks for ages.

'It's the daring young man with the flying machine,' the new arrival grinned, giving her companion a friendly pat on the back. He turned to her, his malt-brown eyes twinkling. 'And you must be Shelly?'

'I am,' she agreed cautiously, for there was something in his smile she did not quite trust.

'Aha! I've been hearing all kinds of intimate details about you, courtesy of one indiscreet gent.'

She flushed. 'I don't know what Pieter's said, but I assure you none of it is true.'

'I believe you,' nodded the doctor, though his nonstop smile made it abundantly clear he did not.

'Is Pieter OK?' David enquired.

The doctor's amusement faded. 'The honest answer to that is, I don't know. From his injuries he appears to have fought a battle with the windscreen. Yes?' he said to Shelly.

'I didn't see the actual collision, but I think that's what happened,' she agreed.

'The impact would have sent a lesser individual straight to the mortuary, but this guy appears to be built of brick. He has some minor abrasions to his head and a bad dose of concussion. Unfortunately, there's a possibility of internal contusions. A faint one,' he emphasised, when she looked at him in alarm.

'Can't you do a brain scan or something, and check?' Shelly asked.

'We don't have the appropriate kind of equipment here.'

'Suppose I fly him over to Antigua?' David suggested.

'I'd be very grateful. Chances are he'll be fine, but I prefer not to take chances. Ideally Antigua should have a look at him as soon as possible,' the doctor said, growing pensive, 'but he'll need supervision during the flight and we're short-staffed. I've dealt with his arm and the ribs he's damaged, so they're no problem, but the guy's restless. Not violent, just tends to ramble and try to fling himself around a bit.' He sighed. 'As there isn't a nurse available, I guess we'll have to keep him here overnight.'

'No need. Shelly'll take charge,' David said immediately. 'She's a trained physiotherapist, so her background is medical.'

The doctor smiled. 'Great. If I can release him into the care of a professionally qualified person, our worries are over.'

'Are you sure you can't round up a nurse from somewhere?' she asked. At David's offer, her mouth had gone dry and she needed to swallow. 'Please don't think I'm unwilling to help, it's just that—that there are two appointments in my diary for this afternoon, one due to start in half an hour,' she said, her eyes going to her watch and staying there. 'I hate to let people down.'

'Give me the names, and I'll ring and explain,' David instructed. 'Whoever they are, they'll understand.'

'So it's all clear?' the doctor enquired.

'No,' she said.

David's look was a hundred per cent exasperation. 'Why not?' he demanded.

Shelly raised her head and began speaking to the doctor. 'Because I don't have a professional qualification. I did three years' training and passed every examination to that date, but—— ' although red flags burned in her cheeks, her voice remained firm '—family matters prevented me sitting the final papers.' She did not look at David. There was no need. She knew he would be furious. She knew he would be thinking how, all along, he had suspected she was a racketeer, and that now he had been proved right. She knew she had hit rock bottom in his estimation. 'My knowledge of anatomy, physiology and behavioural science is extensive,' she continued, more as a boost to her ego than to provide information. 'I'm skilled in therapeutic movement and——'

'You'll do fine. More than fine,' the doctor assured her. 'I'll rustle up an ambulance and arrange for one to be waiting when you land in Antigua. Pieter's been given a sedative, so I don't anticipate too much trouble. I'm in your debt.' He grabbed hold of her hand and shook it warmly. 'Many thanks.'

After farewells, he hurried off.

'Before you say a word,' Shelly said, swivelling to the man beside her, 'I wish to point out that——'

'Leave it. Tell me who you were due to see and——' David held out his hand '—give me the keys for your moke. When I've finished telephoning, I'll take it round to the car park. It'll be out of the way there. Then I'll go and prepare the plane.' In one stride he was at the door. 'See you later.'

Manoeuvring Pieter aboard the aircraft proved to be a test of strength, endurance and ingenuity. Seats had been removed to provide ample room, but the stretcher was wide and the doorway narrow. While David hunkered down and negotiated from inside, the two ambulancemen huffed and puffed on the outside. Sinews strained and muscles bulged, and by the time their load was finally inserted, the three men were glossy with perspiration.

'Grab a seat, sweetface,' David instructed, mopping his brow, 'and let's get this show on the road.'

'Oughtn't I to stay with Pieter until we're airborne?' Shelly said, from where she hovered beside the invalid. A grip was taken on canvas webbing which held the stretcher in place. 'I'll be fine.'

He glanced back over his shoulder. 'Sorry, the rules are that you sit here beside me.'

'Remember the night under the palms?' the Dutchman demanded querulously. His eyes were closed, had been closed during the entire embarkation, but his voice was wide awake and loud. 'Remember——' He struggled to release his good arm. 'Remember the sand on our backs?'

'I remember,' she said. Anything to pacify. 'David, suppose the motion of the plane disturbs him? Suppose he panics? He could injure himself.'

He paused in his inspection of the mass of dials, levers and knobs. 'OK, stay with him,' he said reluctantly. 'But hold on tight, *very* tight.'

'I will,' she promised.

As David began to flick a procession of switches, Pieter opened unseeing eyes.

'Didn't we have fun?' he demanded. He gave a guffaw worthy of a smutty comedian. 'Best fun ever, wasn't it? Bet you never had fun like that with anyone else, did you?' His voice rose in cantankerous insistence. 'Did you, Shelly?'

'Never. Now, sshh.'

But Pieter blathered on, spouting bawdy nonsense and sometimes frowning, sometimes laughing. Enclosed in a world of his own, he remained immune as the propellers shuddered into life, immune to the high-pitched whine of the engines, immune to the tilt of the stretcher as they soared upwards. She smoothed his brow and chanted messages of comfort, though whether anything penetrated was debatable. As they reached their flying altitude Pieter's diatribe suddenly ceased, to be replaced by noisy snores. Now Shelly was able to concentrate on the rehearsal of a speech, because at the first opportunity she intended to make it clear to David that her admission of a lack of qualifications in no way represented a defeat. That, whatever he may think, she had not fallen flat on her back.

'Those nights of steamy passion sound intriguing,' he said, as he hung his headset around his neck. His mouth quirked. 'Are you sure you missed out on them all?'

'Positive!' she yelled, needing to shout because it was noisy in the plane, the drone of the engine overlaid with electronic buzzes and crackles.

He laughed, and nodded towards the seat beside of him. 'Pieter's settled, so would you care to join me? I'd feel happier if you were strapped in, and it'll also be easier on the vocal cords.'

'I know you think I've deceived you and, yes, in a way I have,' Shelly said, starting her speech as she clambered beside him. She fastened the safety belt. 'But the only thing I lack as a physiotherapist is a piece of paper. I did all the practical training, attended every single lecture, and I was top of my year each year. I'm *good* at what I do!'

David held up a hand. 'You're preaching to the converted.'

'I am?'

He grinned at her look of astonishment. 'Hell, I'm not so blind I haven't seen how much fitter Jessica is since you took her over.'

Happiness swept along every vein, exuded from every pore, brought a wide smile. This was the news she wanted to hear.

'You're glad I came out to Nevis to treat her?' Shelly asked.

'I'm delighted. And very, very grateful.'

How far did his gratitude go? she wondered. As far as agreeing to Gail's ownership of the pottery, now and for ever? She longed to believe so, yet held back from asking. The improvement in Jessica's health would continue, so it made better sense to wait until nearer the end of her stay and tackle David then. After all, the greater his delight, the more magnanimous he was likely to be.

'You don't mind that I can't produce a diploma?'

'Nope.' He grinned his tipped-down grin. 'Though it'd be interesting to know more about those family matters which prevented you taking your exams.'

On the point of saying more, he frowned, listened to the engine noise, then adjusted a lever.

'How did you get on with Pearl?' Shelly enquired, making use of the diversion. She wanted to bask in his acceptance of her as a *bona fide* physiotherapist. What she didn't want was to be forced into revelations. She slid him a mischievous smile. 'Did she make advances?'

'One or two.'

'And?'

'I asked her to remove her hot little hand from my knee,' David said, showing an effortless facility for becoming playful.

'It worked?'

'What do you think?' The laughter in his eyes was irresistible.

Her brow knitted as a coughing sound came from one of the engines. 'What's the matter?'

David studied the dials and altered another switch. 'There must be a spot of dirt in the fuel. It's nothing important. Suppose I place my hot little hand on your knee,' he said, doing just that, 'and inform you that we're safe and sound, are you going to ask me to leave you alone or will you be happy about it?'

'As Larry,' she grinned, supremely aware of the touch of his fingers on her bare leg. 'Whoever he happens to be.'

'I understand he was Larry Foley, a noted boxer.'

Shelly laughed. 'How did you know that?'

'Sweetface, I'm ten years older than you.' He raised jokey eyebrows. 'An old man, but also a——' There was a second cough, one which sounded as if it came from both engines. David examined the instrument panel, then adjusted more levers. 'I do have a great deal of experience,' he said.

'Really?' Shelly enquired sassily.

He peered ahead. They were high above the ocean, equidistant between the two islands.

'The reference was to my flying skills. I got hooked at sixteen, that's when I first went up in a glider, and flew solo before I was allowed to drive a car.'

'I don't know why you're telling me all this, but I'm extremely impressed.'

'I should hope so.' He flashed a momentary smile. 'I obtained my commercial pilot's licence as soon as I could,' he continued, 'and spent a long time flying jets for scheduled airlines.'

'Why did you decide to change?' Shelly enquired, realising that their flirtation, for that was what it had been, had ended.

'Being my own boss appealed, but——' The cough—was it in one engine or two?—sounded again. The aircraft juddered. David swore. 'I also wanted to fly something smaller.'

'Is everything OK?' she asked.

'No sweat.' His assurance was hearty. 'The biggest thing I fly now is an old DC-3. I used it to take the donkeys down to Barbados two or three weeks back.'

'Donkeys?' she frowned, then remembered Jessica's reference to stock and Pearl's subsequent grilling. 'You had problems?'

David nodded. 'I'd gone more than half-way with the first batch when one of the friskier individuals decided it preferred terra firma. In its efforts to get free, the bloody thing incited its mates to attempt a stampede. Every single animal moved, which loused up the balance completely.' He let out a breath. 'To describe it as a nightmare is putting it mildly!'

'Were you on your own?' Shelly asked, forced to speak to his profile because his gaze remained resolutely on the instrument panel.

'No. I had a couple of loaders on board, but when the donkeys panicked there wasn't much anyone could do. I'd planned on five runs, but after that it seemed safer to reduce the number of animals airlifted at any one time. The five runs became——' He scowled at a dial and his hands tightened on the controls. 'I lost count.'

Again both engines coughed in unison, and the plane jolted as if flicked by the fingers of a capricious giant. Another cough and another jolt followed. Bodywork creaked, the wings vibrated. David's cap spun from its shelf to frisbee through the air, followed by a clattering clipboard.

'Sorry about that,' he said, as they steadied. 'There must be a fair bit of dirt, but it'll clear itself.' He frowned ahead to where the land mass of Antigua could be seen in the distance. 'We're nearly there.'

'No!' wailed Pieter, all of a sudden.

Shelly spun round. Strapped in like an Egyptian mummy, he remained secure, but his eyes were wide open and distress showed on his face.

'I must go to him,' she said, her fingers busy at the buckle on her safety belt.

David shook his head. 'Not yet.'

'He needs me.'

'I need you in that seat.'

'Please, please,' whimpered the Dutchman.

Ice-axe eyes impaled her.

'Don't you dare move!'

The engines coughed, gagged, choked—and the small plane dropped. Shelly had no idea how far they fell—not far, probably only ten or twenty feet—but it was enough to make her heart knock wildly against her ribs, enough to snatch away her breath, enough to make her *scared*. As Pieter mumbled his need for assistance, David jammed the headphones against his ears and said something indistinct and urgent to the control tower.

'We have landing instructions,' he said, as a disembodied voice uttered an unintelligible reply, 'so I'm going lower.'

'Already?' she queried, for Antigua still looked a long way away.

'Need to be in position for our approach,' he muttered, and took the plane down and down and down. 'Ever heard of St Elmo's fire?' David enquired, sounding like someone at a cocktail party making bright conversation.

Shelly gazed out at the waves which now lapped precariously close beneath them.

'Isn't it some kind of electric discharge?'

He nodded. 'I came across it over Norway once when green flames began licking over the fuselage. Very spectacular. We don't have that kind of thing in the Caribbean. Flying's pretty uneventful here. The distances are short, and——'

'Would you do me a favour?' she demanded.

He jabbed a glance in her direction. 'What?'

'Stop pretending everything's fine and dandy. I know we've hit some kind of problem and I realise Antigua's told you to take evasive action, but I don't need to be babysat, thanks. Despite being younger and female, I am of equal intelligence!'

'Yes, ma'am.' David hesitated. 'I hope the weather continues to behave itself,' he said, plainly playing for time while he decided whether or not to explain. 'We have a provisional booking from four guys from Philadelphia whose aim it is to visit as many islands as they can in three weeks, and we're waiting for them to confirm. If the deal comes off it'll mean dollars in the bank.' The needle on the dial which had been receiving most of his attention suddenly climbed. 'Things are looking better,' he crooned. The needle steadied. 'Things are looking good.'

He was right. There were no more coughs, no more jolts, and they landed without incident. As he helped her down from the plane, Shelly admitted to a wobbliness at the back of her knees—yet David was supremely matter-of-fact.

'I need to shut things down,' he said, when an ambulance drove up and the tricky business of transhipping Pieter got underway, 'but I'll join you at the hospital as quickly as I can.' He squeezed her hand. 'We've made it this far, sweetface, so stay bright.'

If the bucking-bronco flight had had little effect on David, it had had even less on the Dutchman.

He was fast asleep when the ambulance set off, but later he opened his eyes and started to ask sensible questions. What had happened? Where was he? How badly damaged was the car? Shelly answered gratefully and felt far more at ease when he drifted back to sleep. At the hospital, the staff were primed for action. Pieter was hurried away and this time the wait was short. When the doctor appeared, he informed her that his examination had revealed nothing out of the ordinary. Pieter responded to all the usual stimuli and should recover from the blow to his head with no ill effects. His other injuries, however, would keep him in hospital for a few days.

'It's such a relief to know he's in the clear,' Shelly said, when David walked into the entrance hall a few minutes later. 'I've been imagining brain damage and paralysis, and——' again, her legs began to flirt with strange gravitational forces and her voice wavered '—all kinds of grisly scenarios.'

He placed his arm around her shoulders. 'Pieter'll be fine. He's made of strong stuff, like you.'

'Me?'

'The flight we've just been through was enough to give anyone hysterics, but you kept your calm.'

She smiled, and took a deep breath. Whatever the traumas, however wobbly her legs, the day was a long way from over.

'Is the plane fit for us to travel back in?' she enquired.

'Go back now?'

'Aren't we? The doctor said Pieter would be sleeping this evening and in no fit state to receive visitors.'

'Do you really want to hightail it over to Nevis straight away?'

'No,' she admitted.

'Then why don't we spend the night here? That'll enable our nerves to steady, and allow us to call in on Pieter in the morning.'

The suggestion made sense, and Shelly nodded. 'Could you recommend a hotel?'

David grinned. 'You don't need a hotel, sweetface. You can stay with me.'

CHAPTER SIX

As she accepted his offer, Shelly was aware of a frisson. To spend the night under David's roof seemed uncannily akin to taking chances; yet there was no debate. The action-packed hours had left her floundering in their wake. Now she felt exhausted, numb and a little light-headed. Thinking the invitation through and making a wise, which presumably would have meant negative, decision, was beyond her. All that mattered was that she liked David, *this* David, and wanted to be with him. He was warm, friendly and—her heart missed a beat—gave off exciting vibrations.

'When did you last eat?' he enquired, ushering her into the royal blue jeep which, he had explained, he kept on Antigua. He swung in beside her. 'At breakfast?'

'Apart from one biscuit at Mrs Brandy's, yes.'

'Which means you must be starving.' David switched on the ignition. 'Right, our first priority is to get you fed.'

Shelly grimaced down at her blood-stained T-shirt and crumpled shorts. 'No self-respecting restaurant's going to fling their arms open wide when I walk through the door.'

'Who needs a restaurant?'

She made big eyes. 'You dabble in *nouvelle cuisine* as well as flying planes?'

'Don't be so condescending!' David protested, in mock indignation. 'Personally, I've always thought it a damn silly idea that being male automatically renders a person incapable of sewing on a button or boiling water.'

'You're a whizz at domesticity?'

'I wouldn't say that,' he admitted, 'but I can throw a few eggs in a pan and finish up with something edible.' He grinned. 'Prepared to give it a try?'

'If I say no, I have a nasty feeling you might lock me in a room and keep me on bread and water for the next three weeks.'

'That's true.'

Shelly laughed. 'Then—yes.'

David's home was a compact white bungalow, tucked away at one end of a small, palm-filled bay. Reached after a drive through farmland where cattle grazed, it gave the impression of being remote yet was, he told her, only fifteen minutes from both the airport and Antigua's main town of St John's.

'Welcome,' he smiled, leading her beneath an oleander-covered porch.

A tiny hall opened out into an airy living-room furnished with pale greens, browns and white. A sofa and chairs in soft mocha velvet stood mid-centre. On one wall, shelves crammed with books and sepia prints of old planes drew Shelly's gaze, while another housed a teak unit which incorporated television, compact disc player and speakers. There were low tables with jade bowls and

Lalique glass, and earthenware pots of ruby-red begonias dotted around.

'You lied,' she accused, her eyes shining in frank appreciation. 'You *are* a whizz at domesticity.'

As David slid apart panels in a wall of glass, she went with him out on to a wide, stone-flagged patio. Pretty with plants and flowering shrubs, it overlooked the curve of sandy shore.

'I can't claim all the credit,' he smiled. 'Where the colour scheme's concerned, I had a great deal of help from——'

'Your fiancée?'

It was one of those instant, off-the-cuff, arrived-out-of-nowhere inserts which you wished you could recall and cancel. Shelly could have kicked herself. She should have known better. One look at the abrupt tightening of his expression *insisted* she should have known better. When they had dined together David had spoken of many things, yet never about the personal side of his life. That had been relentlessly avoided. He had not referred to so much as a transitory attachment, let alone owned up to having once been on the verge of marriage.

'My mother and my housekeeper,' he said tersely. He placed flat hands on the balustrade and stared out at the ocean. 'Anneka and I did choose the bungalow together, but most of the decoration and furnishing took place after we parted.' A muscle flickered in his jaw. 'I thought Jessica understood that that episode came under the heading of classified information, but I seem to have been mistaken.' He turned. 'Would you tell me what she's said?'

'Jessica's said nothing,' Shelly assured him hastily. She gave an embarrassed smile. 'It was Pieter. In passing, he mentioned you'd been engaged but that the relationship hadn't worked out, and—and how on the rebound your fiancée married a Frenchman.'

'I wouldn't call an informed decision "on the rebound",' he remarked, a serrated edge to his voice. 'Did Pieter's narrative also include the fact that they're now getting a divorce?' She nodded. 'Her husband was a guy in his sixties. Romeo and Juliet they were not. I'll see to those eggs,' he said abruptly.

David was rubbing agitated fingers across his brow. She had not noticed it before, but he looked pale and drawn and troubled.

'Suppose I do them?' Shelly offered.

'Would you?' he said, with more apathy than eagerness. 'Thanks. All of a sudden, I feel beat.' In the kitchen he showed her the food, the hob, and explained which utensils lived where among the pine cupboards and drawers. 'I'll set the table on the terrace, then grab a quick shower,' he muttered, as Shelly began making some coffee. 'Perhaps that'll perk me up.'

As he joined her ten minutes later, David's uniform had been replaced by a short-sleeved shirt and navy shorts. With hair sleeked damply back and his tanned skin gleaming, he looked like a man renewed, yet throughout the meal he was quiet and distracted.

After a few thwarted attempts at conversation, Shelly also fell silent. Being reminded of his fiancée had had a disastrous effect—his brow was constantly furrowed, his jawline tense—but from what, exactly, did his edginess spring? Two years had passed since he had discarded the girl, and in two years attitudes could be modified, overhauled, turned upside-down. Had David recognised how pitiless his behaviour had been and now felt ashamed? Or could he be experiencing a different kind of remorse? Did he regret breaking with his fiancée because he had realised, too late, that . . . he still loved her?

Shelly drank her coffee. She did not much like the idea of David being in thrall—though she shied away from defining why—yet it had to be a possibility. According to Pieter, since the departure of the shapely Anneka his life had been devoid of women—except one who had received short shrift. A replacement did not appeal. To her it seemed strange that such a *vital* individual should choose to tread such a lonely path but, if she wanted verification, hadn't David himself told her an entanglement was the last thing he needed? Shelly brooded. Add his stubborn refusal to speak about his fiancée, and didn't all the arrows point to him being trapped in deep, unresolved emotions?

Suddenly he looked up, making her aware she must have been staring.

'I'm being a pathetic host,' David apologised, jettisoning the spoon with which he had been digging morose craters in the sugar bowl. He gestured through the living-room. 'The door on the right is the spare bedroom, and there's a bathroom en suite. Perhaps you'd like a shower, too?'

The thrum of water against her skin was bliss. Shelly stood beneath the spray for several minutes, not thinking, immobile, simply wallowing. Eventually she stirred herself and moved into action. By the time she reached for the towel and had vigorously rubbed herself dry, her skin glowed, her brown eyes shone. Remnants of exhaustion did remain, yet the shower had been therapeutic. Those disturbing thoughts of David pining had been banished to a remote corner of her mind, and now she felt freshly energised in a devil-may-care kind of a way. As she stepped into her shorts, Shelly grinned. Had she caught a strange virus, or were her surroundings responsible? Lost in grim reverie, her partner had been blind to the splendour of the evening: to the pinks, greys and lavenders of the sunset, to the lap of the crystal-clear sea, to the caressing warmth of the breeze; but her perceptions had been acute. The Caribbean entranced her.

While she had been in the shower, the sun had sunk below the horizon. Outside cicadas chirruped in the dark. Inside lamps had been lit. Twin oases of mellow light shone beside the armchairs, leaving the outer reaches of the living-room in soft shadow. David was sitting on the floor with his legs stretched out, resting back against the sofa. His eyes were closed.

'Still feeling beat?' Shelly enquired.

He looked up and smiled. 'I'm fine. I have a headache, that's all.' He indicated a box of compact discs beside him. 'I was intending to choose something soft and soothing.'

Together they settled on a selection of classic instrumentals featuring ethereal strings and a throbbing saxophone.

'Would you like a massage?' she asked, as he returned from organising the music. 'It often helps.'

David dropped down beside her. 'Sounds like an offer I can't refuse,' he said, with a throaty chuckle. 'Which part of me would you like to begin with?'

Pleased to find him willing to communicate again, she grinned. 'I intend to begin and end with the back of your neck. Though maybe, just maybe, I could be persuaded to work on your——' Catching her lower lip between her teeth, Shelly paused.

'Yes? Yes?' he begged, in extravagant anguish.

'Temples.'

Uttering a laughing expletive, David turned and she knelt behind him.

'Feels good?' she enquired, as she began kneading the muscles at the base of his neck.

'It'll feel better if I take off my shirt.' The buttons were undone, and he cast it aside. 'On you go, sweetface.'

To be presented with him stripped to the waist did strange things to her metabolism. As the massage resumed, Shelly's pulse quickened and her heart lurched into a faster beat.

'All right now?' she asked, consciously needing to keep her voice on an even keel.

His reply was a contented murmur.

For some reason it became important to study the back of his head. Springing thick and glossy from his crown, his dark hair waved in regular arcs to curl around his ears in capricious wisps. At his nape a little downward, temptingly strokable point had formed. Her eyes slid to his shoulders: bronzed and wide, they were the kind on which worlds are carried.

'Aren't you supposed to do this with oil?' David enquired.

Shelly blinked. 'Oil?' she echoed, as though she had never heard the word before.

He twisted round his head and grinned. 'Don't you carry a bottle in that vast haversack of yours?'

'There's—there's baby oil.'

Manipulating muscles which were taut, golden and *slippery* had a devastating effect. Shelly had touched bodies many times before, but they had never felt like this one. As she pushed and eased, excitement began to gather at the base of her spine, began to zizz and flow through her fingertips. Did David feel the current? she wondered. Surely he must be aware of the electricity? Frightened that what she was feeling might only be happening to *her*, she became the brisk, mundane therapist.

'Your muscles are knotted. That's because you work too hard and too long,' Shelly informed him.

'Listen who's talking, *you're* out on your calls from morning until night,' he protested.

'Agreed, but the difference is I pace myself. I make sure there's time to relax, to walk, to swim. When did you last swim?'

David gave a surprised laugh. 'Y'know, I can't remember.'

'According to Jessica, you don't play sports or take much in the way of worthwhile exercise,' she said, rotating her thumbs against his shoulders. 'You're fit now, but if you carry on like that you could drop down dead with a coronary in ten years' time.'

'Gee, thanks.'

'I'm serious, David.' The back of his head received a severe frown. 'If you intend living out your full span——'

'I've been wondering whether to confess to this or not,' he interrupted, 'but I reckon I should, us being equals.' Covering her hands with his, he halted the massage. 'Earlier today there was a grave danger neither of us would live out another hour, let alone three score years and ten. You see, when I reckoned there was dirt in the fuel, I lied. What we were suffering from was electrical failure. I've had one engine go on the blink before, but never two at the same time. The fault was intermittent and, thank God, the electrics started working properly again at the crucial moment, but a guy suffered similar trouble over Trinidad last year and——' his voice was hushed '—he didn't make it.'

Shelly freed her hands and slid them down his chest. As a long-term professional programmed to pilot-passenger ethics, all David's instincts must have rebelled against the admission that their lives had been in jeopardy—yet he had been honest with her. A smile seeped through her body. She knew how much the revelation must have cost.

'Never mind.' She felt like hugging him, but lost her nerve at the last minute. 'We arrived alive and that's all that matters.'

He turned, bringing their eyes, their noses, their mouths, so close she could feel his breath against her cheek.

'You sound amazingly flip.'

'It's reaction to all the tension.'

David gave a wry laugh. 'Great! You hang loose, while I'm felled by the grandaddy of a headache. It came on the minute we touched down and I knew we were safe.'

'That's what's been troubling you?' Shelly asked.

'What else?'

'Nothing,' she said, and happily tossed her 'Anneka' thesis away. 'How's the head now?'

'Almost gone.' David raised his brows. 'See what the touch of you on me can do?'

Any frivolity attached to the words was devalued by the darkening of his blue eyes. Shelly's heart pounded. He had been as aware of the sexual voltage as she.

'Shouldn't we celebrate?' she enquired, in a burst of exhilaration. 'It isn't every day you're snatched from the jaws of death.'

'Good idea. What would you like to drink? I can offer bitter lemon, orange——'

'I'd prefer something stronger.'

'What's happened to your usual caution?' David enquired, looking amused.

'It seems to be somewhere else tonight. And as there was a first time for facing up to a storm, so there's a first time for——' Shelly wrinkled her nose '—white wine?'

He disappeared into the kitchen, soon returning with a bottle and two glasses. 'Does it meet with approval?' he questioned, when she took a trial sip.

'Ask me when I've reached there.' She marked a line with her finger.

David laughed and settled himself down beside her. 'Tell me about your boyfriend. Gareth, wasn't it?'

'You're right; with both the name and the past tense.'

'You regret the past tense?' he queried.

'No, it's just that it still surprises me. Gareth and I first met at school and were together for eight years. Everyone believed we were bonded for life, and for a long time we did, too.' Shelly took a second mouthful of wine. 'But our relationship ran out of steam.'

'Familiarity bred boredom?' he suggested.

'It wasn't that simple. We had good times, even towards the end, but they were only good, they weren't great. And they never had been.' She sighed. 'Gareth was steady, faithful, possessed a high niceness quotient, and I loved him. But I wasn't in love. Maybe I'm a crazy romantic, but as the years went by I had the feeling that somehow I was missing out. I had the feeling there had to be more.'

'So it was you who ended the relationship?'

Shelly nodded. 'Though it wasn't the easiest or the quickest thing I ever did. For months I suggested something was lacking, for weeks I dropped hints that we should call it a day, but obviously I soft-pedalled, because it took ages before the message was read and understood.'

'You didn't do it right.' David gulped from his glass. 'There's nothing to beat the short, sharp severance.'

'Perhaps not,' she agreed, wondering whether he sounded defensive, or regretful—or neither? 'But I'm not made that way.'

His eyes met hers.

'No,' he said huskily.

The word throbbed with meaning, with his vision of her as a soft and caring woman; one who would never resort to such brutality. He caught hold of her hand and raised it to his mouth, pressing his lips against the blue vein in her wrist.

'I like the way you smell,' he murmured. His tongue teased the tender skin, then stroked up to trace slow, sensuous circles in the centre of her palm. 'And I like the way you taste.'

Shelly's awareness of taking chances accelerated. And she wanted to take them. Tonight was no ordinary night. Tonight was hallucinogenic and magical. Maybe tomorrow she would—who cared about tomorrow?

David spanned his fingers on her throat and drew her slowly towards him.

'Would you care to close those big, brown, beautiful eyes?' he asked.

She smiled, drowning in the nearness of him, in the warmth of his gaze. 'If I do, will you be good?'

'No.'

Her lids fell and he kissed her. It was a kiss of gently questing tongue and infinite thoroughness. By the time he released her, Shelly had used up all available supplies of oxygen.

'I almost spilled my wine,' she said tremulously.

David surveyed her outstretched arm and the glass clutched at the end of it.

'Only almost? I am out of practice. Sweetface, there's no rush,' he chided, as she took a hurried mouthful and set the glass aside.

Shelly looked at him and frowned, trying to sort out what had suddenly become conflicting signals. Did he intend to kiss her again, or had it been an isolated incident? If Gareth had devoted so much care and attention to a kiss, he would have been leading somewhere, and quickly.

'Yes,' she said, adrift and uncertain. 'I mean no.'

David's mouth tipped down. 'I am going to make love to you, but not in five minutes flat.' He slid his hand beneath her T-shirt and began stroking his fingertips back and forth. 'You have a beautiful body and I'd like to spend time getting to know it.' He gave a tender smile. 'OK by you?'

'OK by—by me.'

As his hand continued to move rhythmically across her midriff, he gave her another slow, searching kiss—and then another. Shelly felt her nipples pull and harden. He was going to touch her breasts. He *must* touch her breasts. Please, please, she begged silently. Yet, although his fingers seemed to caress every other inch of skin beneath the pink cotton, they avoided the high curves.

David drew back. 'More wine?' he asked.

'What?' A desperate attempt was made to apply her emotional and physical brakes. 'No.'

'I will.'

He refilled his glass, took a deep swallow, then put it aside. 'Arms up,' he said, and when she obeyed he peeled off her T-shirt. Her bra was unfastened and the straps lifted from her shoulders. Every movement was fluid, unhurried, smooth. 'You're delectable,' he murmured. David bent his dark head and as he flicked his tongue—a surprisingly rough and hot tongue—against the straining sensitive peaks, a shaft of sensation struck. 'You like that?' he asked, when Shelly gasped.

'Yes.'

'What else do you like?' Feeling her hesitation, he looked up. 'Darling, this is the first time we've made love and I need you to tell me. Despite having a fair grasp of things, I'm not a mindreader,' David smiled. 'My wish is to give you the best possible pleasure, but how can I do that unless we communicate?'

She gazed at him. 'I—I don't know.'

'Did you and your boyfriend never talk?'

'No.'

'So the sex paralleled your relationship—good, but not great?'

'Not even good at times,' Shelly confessed.

Again he bent his head. She felt the tormenting graze of his teeth against her skin. Again she gasped.

'That pleases you?'

'It does,' she said, whispering in her sexual stagefright.

'You want me to do it again?'

'Yes.'

Taking his time—such sensual, glorious time—David devoted himself to her. He asked more questions, received more answers, and gradually she began to feel more at ease with her sexuality, less inhibited. As well as giving information, there was something excessively erotic about telling him what her body craved.

'Don't stop,' Shelly begged, when eventually he removed his mouth and his hands from her.

He smiled and asked for the oil. Pouring a small pool into one palm, he smeared it against the other and began to stroke her breasts. The touch of his palms created an exquisite agony. Shelly wound an arm around his neck and pulled him close. Her lips parted his and she sucked on his tongue. She had never felt so aroused. Half of her brain was shocked at her wantonness, the other half was lost in rapture.

David grinned. 'You don't want me to be gentle?'

'No. Oh, God, no!'

His hands moved to her hips, to her shorts, to her lacy briefs. As he had caressed her breasts, so he began to caress her thighs. The fire which burned within her flamed within him, and he shed his own clothes. Naked, David eased her down with him on to the carpet. Pressing his hands into the small of her back, he pulled her into him until she felt the swollen heat of his arousal against her.

She began to move, rubbing herself against him, dragging her breasts across the dark body hair which covered his chest. She lowered her head and in a mixture of light biting and kisses, explored her way across his torso.

'My wild, beautiful lady,' David murmured.

Wild? Shelly thought dimly. She had never been wild with Gareth, but then there had never been enough time, then she had never felt so free of restriction, then she had not possessed this pagan need to offer pleasure and to receive it.

A sheen of sweat joined the gleam of oil. Skin slid on skin. Tanned flesh shone and tightened and quivered at a touch. Muttering his need, David straddled her. Deep inside, she felt the latent power of him, the probe. The time for talking had gone. For a moment he rested his head against her shoulder, controlling and quietening, then he began to move in violent, thrusting spasms. Beyond thought, beyond reason, Shelly clung. A long time ago the music had ended. Now, as their passion sped relentlessly towards its finale, the uneven rhythm of breathing filled the room. Wider and wider the circles of pleasure spread until they met in skin-shivering, shuddering climax—and both cried out together.

They slept in David's bed, making love at midnight and again before dawn. Each time new levels of intimacy were explored. Each time both of them had been exultant. The next morning, Shelly came contentedly awake. Her body felt tender and achingly female. Smoothing a hand across the empty pillow beside her, she smiled. Deep in the night, David had confessed to the strain of making slow love.

'But you seemed to be so cool,' she had protested.

'I was on fire! You excited me so much, I damn near fell on you and took you straight away. But I didn't want it to be like that,' he had murmured. 'It mattered very much to me that our first time together should be right.'

Shelly nestled down. He might have said that making love properly mattered, but what he had meant was that she mattered to him. The feeling was heart-stoppingly mutual, she thought, and her smile spread. With David she had found the precious and wonderful 'more' she had always believed must exist, with him she had known complete fulfilment. Her dreams had become reality.

Noises of imminent breakfast penetrated, and she waltzed into the shower and out again. She felt so good about herself, so good about what had happened, so good about what was destined to come next. In the morning light her T-shirt looked decidedly yucky, so she decided to wear one of his shirts. A grey and white striped cotton was chosen. The collar gaped, the shoulders hung half-way down her arms, but at least she felt clean and fresh. If she could cinch the shirt with a belt, it would look much better.

In the kitchen, David was engrossed in the preparation of grapefruit. He had his back to her, so she walked up and slid her arms around his waist.

'Good morning,' Shelly said, rubbing her cheek against his shoulder. 'We communicated beautifully last night, didn't we?'

'Mmm,' he replied vaguely.

'Anything I can do?' she enquired, as he placed the fruit on a tray.

'No, thanks.'

'I hope you don't mind, but I've borrowed one of your shirts. If I could also lay claim to a belt it would——' David had turned. She had imagined he would kiss her, but instead he stood stiffly, his eyes serious. Shelly unwound her arms and stepped back. 'You *do* mind?'

'No.' The bubbling percolator was unplugged, and he nodded towards the table outside on the balcony. 'Everything's ready. Shall we make a start?'

She followed him and sat down. When minutes passed and he said nothing, she frowned. While her preference was to ease herself into the day, she had no objection to exchanging a few words at breakfast; but perhaps David was one of those people who required an hour or two before they became civilised?

Suddenly he glanced at his watch. 'If we leave in half an hour, we can call to see Pieter and be on our way to Nevis by ten-thirty.'

'Are you worried about flying back?' Shelly asked, thinking that this would explain his sobriety. After yesterday, perhaps the first time again in the cockpit had become a problem?

David ran his tongue over his lips. 'No. What does worry me is——' He hesitated. 'Last night.'

'Last night?' she echoed.

'Us becoming lovers will take time to get used to. I don't know how I'm going to handle it.'

A delicate scale inside her toppled. Ready to commit herself heart and soul, Shelly realised she was guilty of a severe misinterpretation.

'Oh,' she said.

'Don't say "oh" like that,' David appealed.

She stared down at the hands which had linked themselves tightly in her lap. Doubtless yesterday's traumas had helped heighten and dramatise what had happened at night—in addition to destroying her moral warning system!—but she had been convinced that he *cared*. Shelly's insides shrivelled. What he cared about was physical satisfaction, albeit for the both of them, while she, the beguiled fool, had confused sex with love. What a cliché! Today David might have fought shy of the short, sharp severance, but the message he gave was readily deciphered.

'Be honest,' she protested, adopting a savage gaiety. 'What you mean is that anyone who bed-hops these days needs their head examined, if not other parts of their anatomy, and you regret the whole thing. Well, if it's any consolation, I don't bedhop. You're only the second man I've ever slept with. In addition, nothing seemed quite real last night, so don't worry——'

'I don't think you heard what I said,' he cut in.

'I heard all right.'

David moistened his lips again. 'Shelly, I don't want anyone to get hurt. I've been down a few more roads than you,' he said heavily, 'and——'

Afraid tears might spring from her eyes at any moment, she was searching for a way to end the conversation when she spotted a brown paper parcel propped up in the living-room.

'What's that doing here?' Shelly demanded.

He gave an impatient sigh. 'I found it on the back seat of your moke and because I didn't like to leave it there, I stuck it in the plane,' he explained, as she rushed to retrieve it. 'Last night, when you were having your shower, I remembered it was in the jeep. I meant to tell you.'

'Mrs Brandy must have dropped it off as we went to help Pieter.'

'Mrs Brandy?' David enquired.

Shelly nodded. 'She insisted on giving me a memento.'

'What is it?'

'No idea. I didn't have a chance to look.'

'Don't you want to look at your memento now?'

The honest answer would have been 'no', for as his interrogation had progressed he had grown wary and sarcastic. The lover was taking up the stance of sparring partner again.

'Let's.' The string was wrenched off and the paper thrust wide. 'I'm sure it was generous of Mrs Brandy,' she said, looking doubtfully down at a dark oil painting of a shipwreck, 'but——'

David had left his seat to stand over her.

'Extremely generous. This was hanging in her house?' he demanded. 'You saw it, told her how much you liked it and persuaded her to part company?'

'Persuaded her? Part company?' There was a moment of incredulity as what he was suggesting filtered through. 'What kind of a person do you think I am?' Shelly protested.

'How many of your other patients have presented you with gifts?' he hit back.

'None! And I resent the implication that I shrewdly go forth, drop heavy-handed suggestions and reap a cornucopia of unlawful goods as a result.' She took a steadying breath. 'For heaven's sake, David, a gloomy old oil painting is nothing to get excited about.'

He jabbed a finger. 'You've forgotten about the signature.'

'G. Ezekiel,' she read. 'I can't recall hearing his name being spoken of in the same breath as Turner, Picasso, Gaugin.'

'You don't know the guy?'

'Regrettably not.'

David scowled. 'He's one of the Caribbean's leading artists.'

'Bully for him.'

'This picture must be worth three or four hundred dollars. I don't know Vanilla Brandy that well, but I do know she isn't rich.' He folded his arms. 'Why would she suddenly decide to buy something as expensive as this and give it to you?'

'I haven't the faintest idea.'

'You didn't realise the——' his eyes were icy '—memento was valuable?'

'How could I, when I've never heard of the painter and, what's more, I hadn't even unwrapped it?' Shelly wrenched back her chair. She could not eat any more breakfast. Her appetite had gone. Another mouthful would choke her. 'You know what really kills?' she demanded. 'It's not you making love to me one, two, three times, then deciding it wasn't such a bright idea after all. It's that you're so quick, so eager, so *adamant* about putting me in the wrong. Not for a second am I allowed the benefit of the doubt—no, the automatic accusation is one of grand sin!' Her voice cracked. 'Ever since we met there's not been a day, an hour, a minute, when your mistrust hasn't sat like a skeleton at our feast. I'd be obliged if we could go and see Pieter now, and I'd also be obliged if you would take that——' Shelly snapped her fingers at the painting '—back to Vanilla, because I never want to see the damn thing again!'

CHAPTER SEVEN

SLIDING his hand into the open neck of his shirt, David began to rub his fingertips across the whorls of dark hair. 'Maybe you're right,' he brooded. 'Maybe I am too distrusting.'

'There's no maybe about it!' Shelly retorted.

'Everyone has their reasons for the way they think, the way they behave,' he said, his voice oddly flat.

'You mean something has happened to make you so judgemental? Huh, I hope it never happens to me!' The back and forth scouring of his chest was hypnotic. She wished he would keep his fingers still. 'Going to tell me what it was?' she challenged.

He frowned. 'No. You wanted a belt. They're on a rail behind the closet door. Take your pick.'

Blonde head held high, Shelly marched away. She grabbed the first belt—a narrow one in black leather—and fastened it around her waist. A few deft tugs, and the grey and white cotton was blousoned over it. Glancing in the mirror, she decided that although her face was scrubbed clean and her hair combed straight, her appearance had gathered a mite of sophistication.

In the living-room, David was waiting. 'Ready to go?' he asked.

Chin raised, she headed for the door. 'Try and stop me!'

They found Pieter propped up against pillows, with his chest well strapped and a neat row of stitches in his head. He was in high spirits.

'I feel fantastic,' he declared, his grin making it plain that yesterday's concussion was already a distant memory. 'The nurses here are the tops. True angels of mercy.'

'Is there anything you need?' Shelly enquired.

He leered at a young sister who happened to be passing the end of his bed. 'Just plenty of loving care.'

'What about visitors? Even though you're only in for a few days, it can be lonely——'

'I have mates on Antigua,' he said, 'but——' The smile he shone at the various nurses up and down the ward was based on the scatter-gun principle: if he spread it wide enough it was bound to hit one of them. 'I'm among friends here.'

'Let us know when you're due to be discharged, and either Ralph or I will collect you,' David told him.

'Thanks.' The offer reminded the invalid of the upheaval he had caused, and he grabbed hold of both their hands. 'I'm so grateful to you for bringing me over,' he said, and went on to give a fervent recital of appreciation. 'Please make my apologies to Mrs Severney, but assure her I'll be back as soon as possible.' After speculating on the difficulties his absence from the hotel kitchen must create, he rallied again. The tea trolley was on its way around, pushed by a lissom black girl. 'Deirdre's planning a visit to Amsterdam next year, so I've told her I'll arrange my leave at the same time and we can travel together.'

'It's time Shelly and I travelled,' David remarked, as the young Dutchman's eyes glued themselves to the approaching tea girl.

'Ya,' he said, with a distracted smile. 'Bye.'

'With Pieter, it's everything to excess and nothing in moderation,' Shelly commented, as they headed for the airport. 'He drives like a maniac, damn near dislocates your hand when he squeezes it, and——'

'Switches from one infatuation to the next faster than a speeding bullet?' David completed. 'You realise you're not going to be *numero uno* when he gets back to Nevis next week?'

'Next week? I had the impression I was already a back number.'

Silence fell between them and, as they motored on, her gaze went to the tanned hands which held the wheel. Those hands, with their long fingers and blunt-cut nails, were the hands which had held *her*, which had spun her up and up to a pitch of pleasure she had never believed possible. She sneaked a look at his profile. That was the mouth which had met hers, so caressingly, so urgently, so—— Shelly's thoughts crumpled. Why spend time dwelling on the intimacy they had shared when she was a back number with David, too? What she must do was what any smart girl would do—chalk up the fiasco to experience. The difficulty was, their intimacy had not seemed like a fiasco. It had seemed like two people making love with caring and sensitivity.

'Last night was pretty... overwhelming,' David announced, out of the blue.

Startled, she shot him a glance. Why say that, *then*? It was as though he had looked inside her head and seen what she was thinking.

'Nobody said it wasn't good while it lasted,' Shelly replied, as flippant as she could be.

He frowned out at the road ahead. 'Sweetface, when I spoke earlier about not wanting anyone to get hurt, I——'

'Would you do two things for me?' she cut in.

'What?'

'Firstly, stop calling me sweetface. And two—shut up!'

Whether her fury silenced him or whether he simply recognised the wisdom of keeping his own counsel, she did not know; but for the remainder of the journey he kept quiet. The next time David spoke was as he drew the moke to a halt outside the airport building.

'Before we leave, I need to have a word with Ralph and a check on the mail. I'll be as quick as I can, but while you're waiting why don't you have something to eat? One way or another,' he said, swinging out of the driving seat, 'breakfast was not such a great occasion.'

As he disappeared through a door marked 'Hawk-Air' in gold letters, Shelly walked along to the main hall. She bought a mug of coffee and a chocolate biscuit at a kiosk, then went and sat down. Judging from the activity taking place around her, mid-morning was a peak period. Tourists in plaited straw hats agonised over what to buy from the duty-free shop. Children played hide-and-seek among the tubular steel chairs. Travellers slumped down, grew bored, sprang to life when their flight was called. Outside, planes landed and took off.

A flurry at the swing doors drew Shelly's attention. A tall brunette had entered and, after pausing to toss back what seemed to be several yards of peat-brown hair, she started to make her way leisurely through the crowds. As she strolled, all eyes followed. In a white silk dress, gold high-heeled sandals, and with a fur jacket draped nonchalantly over one shoulder, the woman exuded 'glamour' from every pore. Aware of the interest she had aroused and taking it as no more than her due, she gestured to the porter scuttling behind. A row of seats had been identified and were to be colonised as her own, and now orders were given, a designer travel-bag and matching make-up valise stacked, a tip handed over.

The woman sat, her split skirt providing tantalising glimpses of tanned thigh, but she was not still for long. Abruptly her slanted brows rose in surprise and she smiled, waved gaily, leapt to her feet.

A friend had been recognised. In conjunction with everyone else—and feeling like a tennis tournament spectator—Shelly swivelled to see who could have inspired such a dazzling smile. Her eyes widened. The woman was running forward to meet...David. He had pushed through the doors and stopped dead, blatantly shocked. In quickfire succession, his shock switched to confusion, wariness, to a troubled tension. Shelly's gaze returned to the woman. Consider his response, and who else could she be but Anneka?

A yard or two from him, the brunette's rush faltered. Had the expression on David's face slowed her? Did she wish she could retrace her steps? Or was she merely deciding what she would say? As Anneka had her back to her, Shelly could not tell; but David's reactions were in clear vision. He said a few brief words, gave a hasty nod of farewell, and looked poised for a quick get-away. But his one-time fiancée had other ideas. She started to talk, and as she did he began to turn the black, gold-braided cap he carried. Round and round the cap went, giving evidence that, whatever it was he was hearing, David did not like it one bit.

Suddenly an impatient gesture batted aside his companion's words, and he came back with *his* point of view. Shelly could not hear what was being said—but actions speak louder than words, and facial expressions louder still. David's jaw had hardened and his blue eyes glittered. Anger was shimmying from him in currents.

'It wouldn't have worked the last time and it won't work now!' he insisted, the phrases suddenly flying out from his onslaught, full-throated and clear.

Foil from Shelly's chocolate biscuit was scrunched up. This morning she had suffered the lash of David's ruthlessness, and had bled. She was still bleeding. Yet here was evidence of his ruthlessness *again*. Shelly's nerves screamed a protest. It seemed incredible that he should have banished such a stunning-looking woman from his life before, but to refuse her a second time—so definitely, so defiantly, and in public—was nothing short of cruel.

The conversation continued, with Anneka issuing a series of appeals until, clearly losing patience, David looked beyond her and began a systematic search of the chairs. When he found Shelly, he grinned. She did not grin back.

'Sorry to keep you waiting,' he said, as he arrived beside her with the brunette, 'but——' his voice and his eyes became cold '—Anneka insisted on a conversation.'

Shelly got to her feet. She longed to assure Anneka that she understood. She longed to explain that she, too, had had firsthand experience of what a bastard David Llewellyn could be. Jilted women of the world unite! she thought fiercely.

'Hello,' she said, her smile loaded with as much sympathy as it could carry.

'I believe some madcap Dutchman had you dashing over hotfoot from Nevis yesterday?' Anneka enquired, showing an admirable composure. One minute immersed in a highly emotional argument, now she was standing with a hand spread on a shapely hip and seemed, if anything, a trifle bored. Her amber eyes swept over Shelly. 'You look as though you were caught on the hop, but I suppose it must have been panic stations?'

'It was.'

Until that moment she had been comfortable with her appearance, but now... Sophistication? What a joke! A baggy shirt was a baggy shirt was a baggy shirt. Next to Anneka she knew she must look the countriest of cousins; all she lacked was a straw in her mouth. It didn't help that David was switching his glance between them. Shelly's temper sparked. Even if he couldn't care less about either her or the brunette, there was no need to draw attention to their differences!

'Shelly didn't panic, though,' he said, 'despite electrical failure hitting us mid-flight. She took the emergency in her stride. She kept Pieter calm. She kept me——'

Anneka ignored his song of praise. 'Where did you stay last night?' she asked Shelly. 'At the Hawksbill Hotel? At Jolly Bay?'

She coloured. 'As a matter of fact——' she began.

'No hotel,' David put in swiftly. 'She shacked up with me.'

Her colour deepened. 'Shacked up' sounded alarmingly loose and laid back and immoral.

'We had dinner, which Shelly expertly cooked,' he continued, as though she had served a seven-course meal which would have had *cordon bleu* chefs slavering, 'and afterwards she massaged away my headache.' He beamed. 'A girl of many talents.'

Shelly began to seethe. She had been wondering why he should want to introduce her to his ex-fiancée, and now she knew. Not satisfied with his blunt rejection, he was using her—as alternative female interest—to hammer the point home. She gave a wry and silent laugh. David had miscalculated. Glamour girls did not rate country cousins as competition!

'Where are you heading for?' she asked Anneka, in a determined attempt to change the subject.

'The UK. I should have left earlier, but my flight's been delayed.'

'I hope you don't have a flight like we had yesterday,' David said, stalwartly returning to what *he* had in mind. 'It was one helluva relief to get to the bungalow.' He placed his arm around Shelly's shoulders and hugged her. 'And an even bigger one to be able to... relax.'

She stood as stiff as a tin soldier. Coming from his lips, 'relax' had been a flagrant pseudonym for 'make love', but how *could* he? Whatever else she thought, she had believed him to be a discreet and private person, yet here he was deliberately making their intimacy common knowledge!

'My divorce becomes final next week,' Anneka announced, showing a blatant disregard. 'I shan't be returning to Antigua unless——' Black lashes fluttered in David's direction and her voice faded significantly.

'Unless someone comes up with a very good reason why you should?' His cap was fixed firmly on his head. 'There's a snowflake in hell's chance of *that* happening.'

If his previous rebuffs had failed to strike, this one knocked flat every single pin. The lipsticked mouth thinned, the amber eyes flashed, and with an irate fling of her fur jacket, Anneka flounced away.

'Thank God!' David muttered.

He took hold of Shelly's elbow and rapidly steered her out of the hall and across the tarmac.

'Is this the same aircraft as yesterday?' she enquired, as he opened the door of a small white plane.

'Nope, that's in the workshop.' He waited until she was installed beside him, then began switching switches. 'This one's been checked and double-checked, so there's no need to worry.'

'I'm not,' she said, but had to admit to a sneaky feeling of relief when their take-off went smoothly.

'Confirmation of the booking with the Americans came through,' David said, as they settled into their cruising height, 'though the trip's been put forward a couple of weeks. Fixing accommodation at such short notice wasn't easy, but it's been done. I leave with them this afternoon.' Strands of dark hair had fallen over his eyes, and he swiped them aside. 'I'd rather someone else did the job, but Ralph's wife's expecting their second child any day now, and the other guys are tied up with the bread and butter trade.'

'Why don't you want to go?' Shelly asked.

He threw her an exasperated look, as though she was supposed to have guessed his reasons.

'Because island-hopping makes it difficult for me to stay in touch. What do you think of Anneka?' he enquired. 'I don't know whether it's because I haven't seen her for such a long time, but to me she looked far too much the powdered and painted movie star.'

If she had been honest Shelly would have agreed, but she would rather walk over hot coals than side with David.

'She's an extremely pretty girl,' she declared.

He pursed his lips. 'I guess so, but——'

'You must have been delighted with the way you manipulated the conversation back there and managed to imply that you and I have some kind of a—a relationship,' she attacked, pent-up resentment suddenly exploding out of her. 'But wouldn't Anneka be surprised to learn that all we had was a one-night stand? And that the only reason that happened was because I had too much wine!'

David gave a disbelieving laugh. 'One glass?'

'Because I don't drink, it went to my head.'

Denying the depth of her emotions—denying *any* emotion—was the only option. How else could she salvage her pride?

'Those few mouthfuls must have been some aphrodisiac,' he said drolly. 'One glass would never——'

'It would,' Shelly insisted. 'I've seen the effects of alcohol. I know how it can lift you out of your skin. I know how it can make you do things you'd never normally do.'

His blue eyes rested on her. 'So when we made love, you were acting out of character?'

'Yes!'

He raised his brows. 'And how did you come by this knowledge of what alcohol can do?' David enquired.

Silently cursing, she readjusted her seat-belt across her breasts. In an effort to escape from one sticky area, all she had done was rush headlong into another. Shelly sighed. Talking about her mother's troubles did not come easily, yet it seemed infinitely preferable to a discussion of her own!

'My mother had a—a drinking problem,' she said stiltedly. 'She wasn't a full-blown alcoholic, but every so often, when life gave her a knock, she'd reach for the bottle.'

'Like when she lost out on acting jobs?'

Shelly nodded. 'When she was sober, she cared about the impression she made,' she continued. 'She was elegant, well mannered, restrained, but when she got drunk she became a giggly loudmouth, and——' another sigh escaped her '—she seemed to make a habit of getting drunk in public. Out of the blue some exasperated barman would telephone, begging me to come and collect her. Whether it was night or day, the pub round the corner or somewhere further afield, I had to go—otherwise she would have ended up spending the night in a police cell.'

David shot her a sidelong glance. 'Was your mother's drinking the reason why you couldn't sit your final exams?'

Among Beatrice's flood of praise, Shelly recalled a comment about her nephew not missing much. The old lady was right. He didn't.

'Yes,' she said ruefully. 'Timing was never her strong point. She'd gone up to London for an audition and been told on the spot that her performance was diabolical. She adjourned to a bar, downed too many gins, and then it was the usual procedure. We have a woman here who says she's your mother, she's being a pain, would you kindly remove her? Unfortunately that involved a train journey.'

'Couldn't Gail have collected her?'

'She was only seventeen, and she hated having to cope with Mum when she was drunk. The staggering around and the noisy hilarity made her skin crawl. When I told the college that I'd been unavoidably called away, they bent over backwards to fix a second date, but——' a hand aimlessly sculpted air '—my mother chose that for her encore.'

David swore. 'Was this something else she didn't bother about too much?' he demanded.

'She did apologise, though with the rider that I'd survive. And I have. I've been able to do everything I've wanted to do in physiotherapy, despite not having a qualification.' Shelly hesitated, then decided that, having gone this far, she might as well go further. 'When I told you my mother slept through the storm it was true, but she was asleep because she'd had too much to drink.'

'Which is why you couldn't rouse her,' he said, frowning at the grim realisation. 'Did she *never* feel any remorse?'

'Oddly enough, yes; in the last few weeks of her life. My mother had no idea she had leukaemia, but for no apparent reason she suddenly announced one day that she regretted having put her career before everything. From then on the "if only" treadmill was walked with a vengeance.' She cast him a glance. 'Many people make the mistake she made, though usually the culprits are male.'

'You mean me?' He squinted ahead to where the airstrip was clearly visible. In a minute or two, they would land. 'I admit my track record isn't exactly fantastic,' he said, when she shrugged, 'but that doesn't mean work's going to be the mainspring of my life for ever more.'

'No?'

'No,' David insisted, clamping the headphones over his head.

Shelly thought of how he had discarded Anneka in favour of Hawk-Air, and how he had discarded *her*.

'I don't believe you,' she said.

He did not hear her.

CHAPTER EIGHT

THE bull's lethargy made a hoof-stamping, nostril-flaring charge seem remote, yet Shelly trod a wide arc. The tethering rope looked worryingly frayed. Eyes fixed on the ponderously chewing beast, she continued her cautious journey. As she reached the ruined church and passed from its sight, she released a breath of relief. Once again, she had been ignored. Yet *El Toro* deserved her thanks, for its presence ensured that the stretch of sand spotted from the moke and long ago claimed as 'her' beach stayed clear of visitors. Shelly's step quickened as she strode down the lower part of the field, the long grasses brushing her legs. Free afternoons were rare, and this one, in particular, would be savoured.

Enticed by the sparkle of the sea, she began a quick strip. First her shirt was shed, next shorts, and finally she kicked off her flip-flops. Now all she wore was a marigold-coloured *maillot*, cut high on the thigh and low at the bosom. A jump down the bank, and her heels gouged imprints in the white, powdery sand. Clothes, bag and towel were flung aside as she ran joyfully into the water. She hugged her arms around her. Heaven was a blue sky, golden sun, and the glide of crystal-clear sea all around you.

Idly she counted. Ahead six, seven, eight brown pelicans floated on the waves, while two contemplated the world from the security of nearby rocks. Lazily one of the birds soared. Wings spread wide, it sailed across her vision and dived into the ocean with a noisy splash. When the commotion had subsided, Shelly turned to scan the narrow beach with its untidy overhang of trees. To her left, the sand strip disappeared around a far corner. To her right, it tapered into a conglomeration of seaweed-strewn boulders. She grinned, pleased with the confirmation that the birds, plus a few white butterflies, were her only companions.

Wading to shore, she pulled down her swimsuit and stepped free. Deftly she dried herself. The towel was spread. Shelly applied an all-over sheen of coconut lotion, then lay back. High breasts, a flat-planed stomach and rounded hips with their dark blonde triangle were offered to the sun's caress. Slowly, inexorably, a purr began to reverberate for, as the touch of the water against her body had delighted, so did the heat. Her mouth moved into a smile. In the past she had never given herself over to such sensual enjoyment, could never have been so relaxed about her nudity. But now, at times like these, she was aware of a confidence and a deep satisfaction. Was the Caribbean responsible for this flowering of the newly vibrant woman she knew herself to be? Or...was it David? Dark glasses were located in her bag. After nearly three weeks spent frantically thinking about everything else *but*, she was not going to dwell on him now.

Shelly polished the lenses on a corner of the towel. Her first act on returning from Antigua had been to volunteer for duty in the Great House kitchens. The desire to help Jessica during Pieter's absence had been spontaneous, yet keeping busy in the evenings had possessed another attraction. It reduced thinking-time. She wrinkled her nose. To be truthful, the success rate in keeping David out of her mind had fallen far short of one hundred per cent. At best, she had struggled through. A tiny yellow crab caught her eye, and she watched as it dug a hole and vanished into the sand. Shelly put on her sunglasses. All she had to do was struggle through for one more day, then she, too, was destined to vanish. Yes, this afternoon must be savoured. It was her last.

'You're leaving early?' Jessica had protested, when she had revealed her travel arrangements the previous day. 'But why?'

'I've taken you as far as I can with the exercises,' Shelly had said, becoming industrious about her knee bends. 'And now Pieter's back. And—and I ought to get home because my other patients need me.'

The latter comment had been an afterthought. Her patients in Wales did not seem real any more. The only reality was the need to exit before David returned from his island-hopping, and that was not so much a need as an urgent obsession. When he had first departed, the three-week breathing space had seemed like a godsend. It allowed her plenty of time in which to recover her equilibrium; or so Shelly had thought. On the next occasion when they met she would be detached, poised and heart-whole. Ho, hum. As the three weeks passed the half-way mark and his days elsewhere began to diminish, so ideas of detachment and poise also diminished. As for her heart, the cracks refused to heal.

That David should have such a disturbing effect was resented. Time and time again, she told herself it made no sense. None at all. How had someone who had shown himself to be a cynical and ruthless careerist *par excellence* managed to get so irretrievably under her skin? Why was she plagued with thoughts of a man who had already hurt her and who, given the chance, could only bring more pain? Panic set in, and hot on its heels came the decision that she must go. Once she reached home, she assured herself, the heart-mending which was proving so elusive in Nevis would begin.

But enough of David. Enough. Shelly stretched and yawned. After a rush-around morning, she felt drowsy. A nearby tree, its boughs reaching down to the sand to form a leafy shelter, offered shade, and she moved her towel beneath it. Lying down, she closed her eyes. The breeze whispered seductively in the palms. The waves rose and fell. A dove crooned. Half-asleep, she became aware of a different sound, a rhythmic beat pulsating up through the sand. She raised her head and gazed blearily out through the lace of greenery. A big chestnut stallion had galloped around the distant corner. Ridden bareback by a golden-limbed man in black swimming trunks, the animal was charging along the water's edge. Spray, like explosions of diamonds, rose from beneath its hooves. The combination of the tropical island shore, a fine horse racing at full speed and the highwayman panache of its rider stirred something primal and thrilling within her, and Shelly sat up to watch. The stallion was relishing each stride, the pull on its muscles, the wind blowing through its mane. As for the man, with dark head bent as he encouraged his mount onwards, he was laughing. Her eyes narrowed. Suddenly she felt throttled. Oh, no! Oh, yes! The laughing cavalier was David!

What was he doing here? Two days ago, so Jessica had reported, he had telephoned from some far-flung isle to advise that he was on schedule, would offload the Americans at the weekend, then continue straight on to Nevis. By the weekend she would have been long gone! Shelly zigzagged from bewilderment to despair to high dudgeon. Folding her arms tightly around her knees, she glowered. He had no right to appear on her beach and cause a disruption. But any disruption would be kept to a minimum. Hidden from view behind the screen of spreading branches, all she had to do was sit tight and he would gallop straight by. How she would cope with a later meeting could be decided after he had gone.

But, as David approached, the gallop slowed into a canter and the canter became a trot. Frightened that somehow her eyes might draw his, Shelly sat with lids squeezed shut and head bowed. He had drawn level with her hiding place when abruptly he tugged at the reins, and swerved into the sea. She could look again. He rode the horse deep and deeper into the water until, in a single graceful movement, he slid from its back and both of them were swimming. A minute or two later, David began sluicing the chestnut-brown back. His purpose had been to wash, but the horse decided they were playing and pawed with a front leg, splashing him tit for tat.

'Whoa there, Prince,' he cautioned.

When his steed whinnied a reply, Shelly grinned. The uncomplicated pleasure of animal and man was hard to resist.

Much cavorting took place before David eventually entwined his fingers in the pale mane and, swimming alongside, coaxed the stallion back to shore. In the shallows Prince shook himself then, submitting to a final spasm of frivolity, reared up on his back legs. In a clumsy, equine waltz, he three-four stepped against the overhang of branches.

'No!' Shelly yelped, scuttling back as hundred-weights of horseflesh suddenly loomed above her.

David grabbed for the reins and drew the stallion back to earth. 'Everything all right in there?' he queried, pushing aside a bough. His eyes widened as they adjusted to the gloom. 'Good God, it's you, Shelly! What are you doing here?'

'Sun—sunbathing,' she stammered, dismayed to find her cover so devastatingly blown.

His mouth tipped down. 'You obviously sunbathe in the same way you make love—all-embracing and no holds barred. Sorry, that was a stupid remark,' he said, when she flushed and hastily crossed her arms over her nakedness. He frowned and retreated. 'I'll tie Prince up in the shade.'

Shelly grabbed for her swimsuit and when he returned she was sitting prim and crosslegged on her towel, applying a fresh coat of coconut lotion.

'What's happened to your Americans?' she demanded, briskly rubbing at an arm.

'I sent them home early, though happy. After twenty islands in almost as many days, they confessed to being somewhat relieved when I called a halt.'

'Why call one?'

David sat down on the sand beside her.

'Because of you.'

'Me?' she queried, her voice rising in surprise. 'You curtailed the trip on *my* account?'

'You didn't think I'd allow you to sneak away from Nevis when nothing's been settled?' he demanded, berating her with a look.

Shelly twisted the cap back on to the lotion bottle. What did he mean? She was well aware her premature departure left one loose end—his agreement to let bygones be bygones where Gail and the pottery were concerned—and it was always possible the reference was to that. Yet an instinctive internal pang warned otherwise.

'I'm not sneaking. I'm departing in a perfectly above board and open way,' she declared.

'At one day's notice?'

'Why not?' Her chin tilted defiantly. 'How did you know I was leaving? Did Ralph pick up on my booking to Antigua?'

'My informant was Jessica. I came across an antique dealer with a Georgian snuff box for sale, so I rang last night to see if she'd be interested. When I asked how you were, I was told you had your damned suitcases packed!'

'She never mentioned that you'd called.'

'I asked her to keep it a secret—as you intended to keep your departure a secret.' David thrust the accusation in like a knife. 'I arrived back a couple of hours ago, all primed to talk.' He paused. 'About us.'

The pang became a cramping.

'A-about us?' she faltered.

He nodded briefly. 'You and me. Together.'

She felt shaky. Fevered. The doubts he had harboured about him coping with their being lovers had, it seemed, been rationalised, mastered, were gone. So, what now? Did he intend to quote the splendour of their one night as a reason for joining forces? Was he going to insist he cared? As his sparring partner she had successfully fought his anger, but could she fight against his love? She bit down hard on a quivering lip. She must.

'Jessica reckoned you hadn't any appointments, so I looked for you everywhere at the Great House,' he continued. 'I searched the grounds. I walked the full length of the beach. When I drew a blank, I remembered your comments about me needing to relax. At that point in time they seemed remarkably apt.' He gave a dry laugh. 'It's funny, it's months since I visited the stables, yet the moment I mounted Prince again I recognised an affinity. Like the one which exists between Beatrice and your sister.' His blue eyes locked with hers. 'Like the affinity which exists between you and me.'

'About Mrs Wilkins and Gail,' Shelly said hastily. 'I can understand why you should feel that your aunt's generosity was ill-advised and premature, but they do have a remarkably *solid* relationship. Also, Gail's determined to make the most of the chance, and is working as hard as she can. The investment won't be wasted.' A leaf was plucked from one of the low branches and flattened in her palm. 'Please, can't you accept that Mrs Wilkins gave her the pottery out of straightforward friendship and that now it belongs to her?'

'I can and I do.'

His agreement came so rapidly and so readily, she blinked.

'You mean that?'

'Sure.'

'There won't be a court case?'

'Nope.'

'Never?' she checked.

David grinned. 'Never ever. I'll put a disclaimer in writing, if you wish.' His grin faded. 'As you said, the idea was hot-headed. I didn't mean it.'

Shelly shredded the leaf in her hand and yanked off another. 'Not even at first?'

'No. The only reason I threatened you was because——' He sighed, and started again. 'For two years now I've been walking around with a boulder-sized chip on my shoulder, which meant that all Beatrice had to do was mention your sister's name and instantly I marked her down as an undesirable. I mean, I *knew* Gail was up to no good. So when Beatrice then went on to tell me about the pottery I didn't exactly foam at the mouth, but it was a close thing. The fact my aunt was entirely happy didn't matter. I resolved then and there to rescue her from her mistake, which meant getting the money back if it killed me.'

Shelly dispensed with a second handful of leaf tatters.

'The bruiser who marched into the studio that afternoon was an avenging angel?' she enquired pertly.

He placed his hand on her arm. 'Sweetface, I don't usually go around yelling at people, believe me. It was just that when I found you there looking so gorgeous and so *innocent*, I—well, I had great difficulty getting my mind around it.'

'I don't blame you for being suspicious,' she admitted. 'When Gail first met Mrs Wilkins, several shady characters sidled up and said—nudge, nudge, wink, wink—the old lady's ripe for the plucking.'

'For a woman of so many words, it's surprising how rarely "no" has featured among them in the past,' David agreed drily.

'Gail warned her to be careful with her money,' Shelly said, rubbing her arm. He had removed his hand, yet the phantom pressure of his fingers remained. 'Then she goes and finances her!'

'Didn't you agree?'

'No. I was abroad when the transaction took place, and I'm sure your aunt waited until I was out of the way.' Several small round fruits grew among the leaves and she wrenched one off. 'Did you return the painting to Vanilla Brandy?' Shelly asked suddenly. 'I've only seen her once since Pieter's accident and neither of us mentioned it.'

He shook his head. 'There wasn't time three weeks ago, so I left it with Jessica. Funnily enough, when I saw her earlier this afternoon she confessed that she'd sneaked a look.'

'And?' Shelly said, when he hesitated.

'It appears G. Ezekiel is Mrs Brandy's second cousin and——' he gave a shamefaced smile '—has been known to present her with examples of his work.'

'So Vanilla hadn't bought the painting!' she exclaimed delightedly.

'No.' David sat straighter. 'I owe you an apology. The accusations I made about the damn thing were... but after spending the night in each other's arms... after a wonderful night... *you* were wonderful.' He had begun speaking in fits and starts. 'When I saw what seemed like proof that you weren't... I just... I felt deceived... cheated... like death... I wanted to... Oh, God! I really screwed up.'

'Your apology is accepted.'

'Thanks. And thanks again for coming to help Jessica with her arthritis. You've restored my faith in human nature.'

'I didn't come out of the goodness of my heart. I came to—to try and *soothe* you,' she protested.

David grinned. 'And you have.'

'You're not worried about the twenty thousand pounds?'

'Frankly, my dear, I couldn't give a damn. Quote. Unquote.'

Milky liquid had oozed from the fruit, and Shelly scratched at her palm where it had made a sticky patch.

'So blasé? You surprise me.'

'If it's any comfort I surprise myself, but I've been the archetypal critic for far too long. OK, we've agreed that with some of Beatrice's associates there were genuine grounds for complaint, yet even if my view was justified there have been many occasions when it was distorted.'

'Like now!' The sticky patch had begun to itch, so she scrubbed her hand against her legs. 'Be honest, David, you must have some sneaky regrets about all that money being lavished on Gail.'

'Why? Beatrice sure as hell doesn't regret anything. The only one who may is Miriam.'

'Miriam?'

'Harold's niece. She's the one who gets what's left when Beatrice shuffles off this mortal coil.'

'No,' Shelly objected, frowning down at palms which had become hot and stingy. 'Miriam isn't——'

All of a sudden he noticed her discomfort and glanced at the low hanging branches of the tree.

'Damn! Got a handkerchief?' David demanded.

'In my bag.'

'I'll get it,' he barked. 'Wipe your hands,' he ordered, thrusting a white cotton square at her. 'Do between your fingers. Much irritation?' he asked, as she sawed away.

She held up her hands and grimaced. Both palms were red and inflamed. 'A fair deal.'

He swore again then, scrambling to his feet, he caught hold of her shoulders and drew her upright.

'Into the sea,' he instructed, flicking the handkerchief away. 'Hold your hands away from your body and move it! Didn't I see you rub your legs?' David questioned, as he bundled her towards the water. 'Have you touched your face? Or put your hands anywhere near your eyes?'

'Uh—no,' she said, bemused by his urgency.

'You're certain?' he demanded.

'Almost.'

'So you could have done?' He led her through the shallows and on, until the water swirled around their waists. 'God! After all the time I've lived in the Caribbean, I'm fool enough to sit by and let something like this happen,' he muttered, berating himself.

'Like what?' Shelly asked. 'What are you——'

He cut her short. 'Take a breath. Now, down!'

A hand clamped itself at the back of her head and she found herself being unceremoniously dunked beneath the waves. His action had by far outstripped her reaction, so when she rose to the surface she was coughing and spluttering. The time under had only been a second or two, but the shock value was sufficient to make her pink-faced and indignant.

'What do you think you're playing at?' she protested.

'Don't!' David snapped, as she went to lift dripping blonde strands from her brow. He pushed back her hair himself. 'Were your eyes open? If not, make sure they are this time. OK, *again*.'

Before she had time to object, Shelly was propelled down into a watery world where sun filtered through aquamarine to highlight a dazzling piece of white coral.

'I had my eyes open,' she gasped, coming up for air.

'Once more, and this time blink.'

Down she went. Up she came. 'I blinked, I blinked,' she rattled off, when he parted her sodden fringe.

A nod of approval was granted. 'Good girl. We were sitting beside a manchineel tree, and its sap is poisonous and highly caustic,' he explained. 'It can cause nasty blisters. Get some in your eyes and it's very dangerous.' His blue eyes swept down. 'Take off your swimsuit.'

'I beg your pardon?'

'Take off your goddamn swimsuit,' he repeated, his voice strongly laced with irritation.

'David, I don't think——'

'Some sap may have soaked into the material, so it needs to be well rinsed. Which is impossible with you inside it.'

'But——'

'We have, as you once reminded me, made love one, two, three times. So your stripping off is no great shakes.'

Not sure whether she appreciated having her nakedness dismissed in such indifferent tones, Shelly peeled down the marigold cloth. Her feet were lifted from the seabed and she floated for a moment until her ankles were free. As matter-of-fact as she could be, she shook the swimsuit, rinsed and pummelled and swished.

'Satisfied?' she demanded.

David caught hold of the water-logged garment and tugged, jerking her towards him.

'Yes, with the rinsing. No, otherwise. I was wrong about you stripping off, it's caused one helluva vibration on my personal Richter scale.' As his gaze fell to the wet-sleeked skin of her shoulders and the tempting swell of her breasts, his intonation grew husky. 'Shelly, I never intended it to happen, but somewhere along the line I've fallen very much in love with you.'

Love? Her breath stopped in her throat. She knew all about his kind of love, she thought despairingly. It was of the 'leave 'em in the lurch' variety. Grabbing the swimsuit from him, Shelly launched into a splashy breaststroke. She needed all the mobility she could muster because, no matter how much her heart might argue, her head insisted she must not be beguiled.

She was swimming as fast as she could, yet it only took a few long-armed strokes to bring him up alongside.

'When we were at the bungalow——' David began.

'I'm not interested.'

His hands closed around her waist, preventing further flight.

'Liar,' he grinned. He lifted her up and around to face him. 'You were very interested, and you still are. And once I've explained, once we've talked——'

'Would you kindly let me go?' Shelly demanded, shovelling hanks of dripping hair from her eyes.

'You have a drip on the end of your nose.' His grin widened. 'Want me to lick it——'

'Let me go, now!'

He sighed and spreadeagled a hand on her back. 'Put it this way—no.'

Like a fiend she batted against his shoulders, but he held her tight.

'I would like to put my swimsuit *on*,' she informed him snootily.

'And I prefer you with it off,' David replied, his smile tweaking with carnal knowledge.

Shelly glared. All her protests, all her pushes and shoves were proving to be academic; brute strength held sway. But she could not remain in his arms with her naked breasts pressed against his chest, with her thighs against his thighs, with both of them becoming hopelessly aroused. Where fearful anticipation was concerned, thunder and lightning were child's play.

'David,' she said, summoning up a fierce kind of dignity, 'this may seem like a game to you, but——'

'No game. I love you and I want to make love to you.' A brow quirked. 'Or hadn't you noticed?'

'And what happens after that?' she demanded. She gulped in a breath. No matter how difficult, there were questions which needed to be asked. 'You propose? We fix a date for the wedding? A wonderful future's planned?' Another breath was taken. 'Then—heigh-ho!—you give me the elbow?'

A shadow crossed his face. 'No,' he insisted, and loosened his grip.

Shelly twisted free. One leg was thrust into her swimsuit, then the other. A swift pull, and she was respectable once more.

'Look, I watched you turn Anneka down three weeks ago,' she said, making for the shore. 'Turn her down flat!'

He gave a strangled laugh. 'It was the only way.'

She stopped and turned to him. 'But that's the second time you've ditched the poor girl,' she said bitterly.

David shook his head. 'No, it's not,' he said. 'It's the first.'

CHAPTER NINE

'THE first?' Shelly's brow furrowed. 'You mean——'

'Anneka was the one who called off our wedding.'

She stared at him. 'But—but why did Pieter tell me it was you?'

'Because that's what he believes. You see, Pieter, like most other people, only has access to the public version of what happened,' David said, striding up the beach beside her. 'The private one—the truth—is different. And for the record,' he continued, 'Anneka is not a poor girl; my definition would be a first-class bitch. Which is why I had no hesitation about turning her down at the airport.' His mouth tightened. 'She and I don't have a single meaningful point of contact. We never did. We never will.'

Shelly lifted the towel and began drying her hair. 'You were going to marry her,' she protested.

'I had a lucky escape. After you've finished, do you think I could grab a quick rub-down?' When she handed over the towel, David seesawed his back dry, then rubbed at his chest. 'Why don't we sit over there,' he suggested, indicating a shady spot well away from the manchineel tree, 'and I'll tell you the whole sorry tale? I first met Anneka when we were on regular flights from Scotland to North America,' he said, as they settled themselves down. 'The international air crew routine—spending a few days here, a few days there, always on the move, always together—can be a fertile breeding ground for affairs. And if a stewardess has an affair with the captain—wow, there's status! From the start, our relationship was conducted against a rarefied and essentially superficial background.'

'Of what?'

'Luxury hotels in Toronto and Boston, and much of the same back in Scotland. As a single guy earning a high salary, money was no object,' he said wryly. 'I lived in style, ran an expensive sports car, used to go skiing, touring, wining and dining, you name it. Anneka loved the life-style,' he drawled. 'However, she didn't love the fool who provided it—me.'

'She must have done!' Shelly burst out and immediately flushed. By insisting that his fiancée *had* to have loved him, wasn't she revealing her own feelings? Hurriedly she found a comb and began untangling her hair. 'If Anneka was happy to become so involved, then it follows that she must have cared,' she stated.

'It was the image she cared for. She never knew the real me,' David rejected, with hard-eyed certainty. 'We were several months into our affair,' he continued, 'when Ralph and I decided to quit the airline and set up our own company. We'd been kicking the idea around for quite a while, but this time it gelled. Straight away Anneka denounced us as nuts, but eventually she came round. Ralph and I talked out our dreams so often, I guess we convinced her Hawk-Air would be an overnight success.' His smile was droll. 'We almost believed it would ourselves.'

'Things didn't turn out like that?'

'No.' David had been watching her comb her hair, and he reached out a hand to tuck one last blonde wisp behind her ear. 'Now you're perfect,' he murmured.

At his touch, her heart had stopped. She loved the way his voice had softened. She loved the way his eyes smiled. She shifted restlessly. Dared she love him?

'So what did happen?' Shelly enquired.

'Well, Ralph and I had liquidised our assets, negotiated a hefty loan, and bought a couple of second-hand aircraft. A fair amount of interest had been drummed up in advance, so when we started some regular bookings did come our way. But competition was fierce, and whereas other operators could afford time with wheels on the ground, for us every minute out of action meant a minute out of pocket. Basically we were undercapitalised. We cut our personal cost of living to the bone, sweet-talked the bank manager again, and held our breath. After a lean patch which kept us gnawing at our knuckles for months, business gradually began to pick up.'

'Anneka was still in Scotland at this stage?'

'Yeah. When Hawk-Air first started I'd suggested she should come out to the Caribbean and work for us, with us, but she wasn't interested.'

Shelly frowned. 'Why not?'

'I imagine being involved at the hard graft, nuts and bolts stage didn't appeal,' he said, with a twist of a lip, 'although Anneka never admitted as much. Instead she waffled on about how she was on the brink of promotion, mentioned a holiday she had planned, and was generally unresponsive. So I left everything open. If I'd had any sense, that's the way it should have stayed,' he reflected cryptically.

'Had you discussed anything—permanent?'

'Not at that point. Fine, we'd spent some good, living-it-up-type weekends together, but I wasn't of the opinion good weekends necessarily lead to good marriages. Or rather, it wasn't my opinion *then*.' David's laugh held no humour. 'But when I came out to the Caribbean and looked back on our relationship, it took on a different glow. What you have to remember is that here I was struggling to get by on a shoestring, feeling as anxious as hell, while in Scotland my greatest worry had been which brand of champagne to choose—almost. In contrast, my life there seemed so satisfactory, and Anneka was a part of it. I forgot she'd never been more than a fun girl with a taste for expensive living, and instead built her up in my mind as a steady, loving, loyal soulmate.' He grimaced, scouring his brow with the heels of his hands as he relived the error. 'The minute Hawk-Air's fortunes took an upswing, I jumped on a plane and went to propose. Anneka said yes.'

'There was no waffling, then?' Shelly asked.

'None. She packed in her job and joined me a couple of weeks later. I was delighted, even though her speedy arrival had knocked my plans for six. When I explained that it would take a month or two for us to fix a marriage licence, buy a house, organise a date, Anneka said it didn't matter, that she would find a way to fill her time. She did.' David's voice reeked with scorn. 'She spent it deciding just who would make the best meal ticket. You see, she now had Philippe in her sights.'

'The Frenchman?' Shelly said in surprise. 'But she'd agreed to marry you.'

'Anneka wouldn't allow a little commitment like that to get in the way. Mind you, I assume that at the time she accepted my proposal I was ahead on points.' He paused significantly. 'But that was before she set foot on Antigua.'

'And then the point-count fell? Why? You were still the same person. And as far as business went, Hawk-Air had survived the lean times and was beginning to come good.'

'The operative word there is "beginning",' he said harshly. 'Yes, we were at last making money, but we were still a very long way from rolling in the dough. And if Anneka didn't care for the demise of my affluence, neither did she appreciate the demise of my status. To her I was *not* the same person. From being escorted by the big fish from the big pond she was kicking around with a minnow from a puddle. Big deal! The signs of her disenchantment were there, if only I'd had the wit to read them. Must the bungalow be so small? Couldn't I afford snappier transport? She didn't care for eating in, it was more fun to eat out.'

'She knew the situation would improve,' Shelly protested.

'I'd told her so endlessly,' David agreed, 'and I believed she had accepted my assurances. We went together to see the minister. She arranged for her family to come out for the wedding. She started buying her trousseau or, to be more accurate, she patronised the most exclusive boutique on the island and left me to pick up the tab.'

Her brown eyes opened wide. 'You paid for her clothes?'

'Plus shoes, handbags and a hundred and one other items. Anneka's one of those women who believes shopping is good for the soul,' he remarked dourly. 'It had been a feature of our relationship that she'd show an interest in window displays and, yuppy-do, I'd be landed with reaching for my wallet.'

'And you called Beatrice a pushover!'

'Dumb, wasn't it? No other woman I'd ever been involved with had expected me to fork out right, left and centre, but Anneka regarded it as her due.'

Shelly tilted her head. 'Did you?'

'I felt she was taking a liberty, but I had plenty of money, so——' A hand lifted in wry acceptance.

'You didn't have plenty of money in Antigua.'

'No. At the time she was breaking all records as the boutique's best customer, Anneka's bank account must have been far healthier than mine,' David said soberly. 'As the ceremony approached, everyone remarked on her eagerness to become a bride,' he said, his expression tightening. 'She was eager. Yet there was a discrepancy; the bridegroom had ceased to be me. Three days before we were due to exchange our vows, she——'

'Three days?' Shelly protested, in horror. 'Pieter said the ceremony was called off at the last minute, but I assumed he was talking in terms of weeks, not days.'

'There were seventy-two hours to go when Anneka dropped her bombshell.'

'But why did she leave it so late?'

'Embarrassment? Lack of courage? Or maybe it genuinely was a last-minute decision?' He moved his shoulders. 'I don't know.'

'She could have told you earlier!' Shelly said indignantly. 'She *should* have done.'

'But she didn't tell me, not in person. The first indication I had that something had gone wrong was when I came up against a contemporary of my mother's, a woman who'd always been extremely friendly.' David moistened his lips. 'What I ought to explain is that, in the weeks leading up to the wedding, I'd spent a lot of time away. Ralph and

I used to take turns doing the overnight jobs, but we'd agreed that I'd cover them in total before I got married, while he'd take over for an equivalent period afterwards. For Anneka and I to start our lives together with me home each night seemed like a guarantee we'd set off on the right foot.' He grimaced. 'I suggested she should come with me on the overnighters. I wouldn't have been working twenty-four hours a day and, in addition to us being able to spend more time with each other, it would have enabled her to get to know the Caribbean. But she rejected the idea out of hand.'

'Why?'

'She reckoned her time was too fully occupied with wedding preparations to consider jaunts.' He fell silent for a moment, then roused himself. 'It was on my return from a night away that I met the family friend. I'd crossed the street to say hello, but before I could open my mouth the woman started bawling me out. Didn't I realise people came before profit? she demanded. How could I bring Anneka out to a strange land and drop her cold? She'd heard of workaholics, but she'd never known how truly selfish they were. On and on she went, at the top of her voice. Passers-by stopped to listen. Traffic slowed to discover the cause of the disturbance.' David shuddered at the memory. 'It took me ages to grasp what she was talking about, but eventually I realised that Anneka had written to each and every one of the guests advising them that the wedding had been cancelled. The woman didn't have her letter with her—thank God, because she'd probably have read it out to the crowd and got me lynched—but it was along the lines of my having decided business came first, so pack your bags, Anneka, and hit the road.' His blue eyes were cold. 'I drove straight to the bungalow to find *she* had hit the road, leaving me a letter of my own. In it she stated that she'd realised Hawk-Air was my first and only love—the succession of overnighters were quoted as proof—and therefore she saw no alternative but to go.'

'She knew why you'd had so many nights away,' Shelly protested. 'She knew——'

'Anneka knew the entire situation,' he rasped, 'but by that time she also knew Philippe could offer her a far superior financial deal. In my innocence I assumed she'd flown home, but news travels fast on a small island and I quickly discovered that the abandoned bride had sought sanctuary at Philippe's club.'

'Anneka had walked out on you and gone straight to him?'

'Stirring stuff, eh?' David said sardonically. 'Stick around, there's more. The moment I learned where she was I went to see her, but I'd barely walked into the entrance hall before the proprietor strutted forward on his built-up heels. When I stated my business, he officiously informed me that Anneka did not want to be disturbed. *She* didn't want to be disturbed?' He gave a strangled laugh. 'She'd cancelled our wedding and told everyone I was to blame, and now she expected me not to bother about explanations but to leave quietly the way I came? I said hard luck, *monsieur*—or words to that effect—if I wanted to visit one of his guests that was precisely what I would do. Philippe adjusted his diamond tie-pin and ushered me into his office, where he took great delight in informing me that, far from being his guest Anneka was, in fact, his *amour*.' The cracking of knuckles indicated that the memory still disturbed. 'I had no idea they'd even met, let alone had any kind of—arrangement.'

'Anneka hadn't mentioned him?'

'Not once. Philippe charged an arm and a leg for so much as a hamburger, so she'd never been to the club with me. I looked at the short, fat pomposity who was making this ridiculous claim, and I started to laugh. But his story of them meeting in the States and how interested Anneka had been to hear about his club soon wiped the smile off my face. He said he'd been delighted when she had appeared in Antigua and started to spend so much time—day and night was implied—with him.'

Shelly frowned. 'So Anneka had turned down the overnight trips in order to visit him?'

'My absences couldn't have suited her better,' David acknowledged curtly. 'Likewise the way I'd obligingly financed her trousseau. To trot round with Philippe's set it was essential she dressed in the latest fashions. It took a few minutes for all this to sink in, but then I realised I'd been well and truly suckered.' Another knuckle was cracked. 'I started to warn the guy that his *amour* was a gold-digger, but Anneka had already planted a character assassination. Like the wedding guests, he believed what he'd been told: that she was all sweetness and light, while I was a villain.'

'But if you'd explained——' she started to say.

'I might have got through to him,' he conceded, 'but I was too choked up to argue, and so when Philippe objected I simply turned on my heel and left. Less than a month later, he and Anneka were man and wife.' David gave a bleak laugh. 'Now he's been taken to the cleaners, poor sod. I understand she's demanded her pound of flesh, and then some.'

'I can understand your reluctance at the time, but why didn't you put the record straight later?' Shelly appealed.

'In part because name-calling isn't my scene, but mainly because I wanted to shut the whole thing out of my mind. Of course, I didn't. I couldn't. I've always accepted that it's an imperfect world, but you can't imagine how *wounded* I felt. And isolated. And angry. And guilty.'

'Guilty!'

David sighed. 'I recognised that there'd always been an emotional gap between Anneka and me, and for a time I hit myself around the head wondering where I'd gone wrong. Then I wised up.'

'Does Jessica know what happened?'

He nodded. 'My family know the truth, plus a few close friends.' He shot her a glance. 'And now you know, that's enough for me. The irony is that, although Hawk-Air had mattered before the split, afterwards I became hypermotivated, which gave credence to the idea Anneka had circulated—that I was a single-minded bastard, engraved to the bone with the work-ethic. In fact, the reason why I dedicated every waking minute to the company was that it seemed safe.'

'Safe?' Shelly queried.

'Hawk-Air demanded my physical and mental energies, but it didn't mess around too much with what happens——' he tapped his chest '—in here. For a long time, much too long, I suppressed my emotions. I felt such a total failure where my private life was concerned; it was the only way I could survive.' His mouth tipped down. 'I guess I was suffering from what the shrinks call an "attitude problem".'

'Anneka should have had the decency to tell you herself she intended to marry Philippe,' she said, fiercely indignant. 'The way she distorted everything and never bothered about your feelings or your reputation is abysmal!'

'I love to feel the heat of your anger—when it's not directed at me,' David teased, then became grave. 'My theory is that Anneka herself found it hard to face up to her two-timing, so she produced the idea of my being work-obsessed in order to justify her behaviour—both to herself and everyone else.'

'There was no need for her to send out those letters!'

'She feels bad about them, too. I bumped into her about a year later and she made a great point of telling me how, once they were in the post, she regretted them.'

Shelly frowned. 'Did that mean she regretted not marrying you?' He nodded. 'Anneka said so—then?'

'She did.' When she continued to look at him, he sighed. 'You want the "i"s dotted and the "t"s crossed?'

'Please.'

'Her suggestion at the airport that we start over was the finale to a campaign she's been waging for quite a while,' he said wearily. 'The first time she voiced her regrets I murmured something about it being water under the bridge, all's well that ends well.' He raised a brow. 'You know, the usual witty, original and decisive stuff. I thought that'd be that. But she's collared me three or four times since, and on each occasion she's spoken about us getting back together.'

'What about her husband?'

'He wasn't mentioned.'

'Good grief!'

'My reaction entirely—except stronger,' David observed. 'When I heard about the divorce, I assumed Anneka would waste no time in leaving Antigua. If I'd thought about it at all recently, which I haven't, I'd have said she had already gone.

So when I walked through those swing doors and saw her waving, I didn't know what the hell to do—short of making a run for it. I desperately tried to think of a way to avoid what I knew she intended to say, but before I'd got out more than a couple of sentences——'

'Something witty, original and decisive about the weather?'

'You're getting the hang of it,' he agreed. 'She started telling me that now she was free, so there was nothing to stop us taking up where we'd left off. And, to top things off, she suggested that, instead of boarding her flight, she could just as easily move into the bungalow!' He winced. 'I pointed out a few salient facts. Like how she'd done the dirty on me. Like how any feelings I'd had for her had vanished in the haze of time. Like how getting together held no appeal. I laid it on the line, but she was too thick-skinned. And too determined. I decided that the only way to prove I had no intention of allowing her back into my life was to introduce her to you and to make it plain we were lovers. I realise you didn't like me telling her——'

'I hated it!'

An apologetic fingertip was rubbed along her arm. 'I hated it myself, but I didn't know what else to do.'

'If you had to introduce us, I wish it could have been at another time,' Shelly sighed.

'Why?'

'Because Anneka was decked out as the princess, while I felt like the pea!'

'Rubbish! Seeing the pair of you together just emphasised what I've always known: that Anneka's appearance, mannerisms, everything she says and does, are totally contrived. Whereas you,' David continued, never taking his eyes off her, 'are genuine and natural, both in person and in bed. They say someone who's passionate about ideas is usually passionate when it comes to love, and——'

Shelly interrupted him. 'What ideas am I passionate about?'

'Making recompense for Beatrice's handout.' He laughed. 'You know, when we first met I was convinced you came equipped with horns and a tail.'

'As you made very plain!'

'Want me to grovel?'

'Please. Hey, what are you doing?' she protested, as he put his arms around her and pulled her down with him on to the sand.

'Throwing myself on your mercy—or something like that.' David spread his hands on either side of her head and kissed her, his tongue deep inside her mouth. 'I said earlier I wanted to make love to you, and I still do.' His hand was raised to her breast, where he caressed the burgeoning nipple. 'And you want us to make love, too.'

Shelly pushed herself out of his embrace. She could not deny the truth of the words, yet there was a matter which needed to be clarified—a matter which could change everything.

'About the twenty thousand pounds——' she began, as her spirits suddenly drooped.

He groaned. 'We've been through all that, so can't we just forget it? Can't we concentrate on what matters?'

He did not need to say what it was that mattered, the seductive stroke of his blue gaze down her body said it for him.

'This is important,' she insisted.

With a sigh, David pushed himself upright. 'Go on,' he said, in the tone of the long suffering.

'You have your facts wrong about who'll eventually inherit Mrs Wilkins' estate. It isn't Miriam.' She gulped in air. 'It's *you*.'

His brows drew together. 'But I understood that——'

'Three years ago Miriam married a stockbroker.'

'I know,' he said, before Shelly could get any further. 'I've only met the woman once, but Beatrice mentions her in her letters to Jessica and occasionally news filters through.'

'But did you also know that at the end of last year her husband made a spectacular killing in property shares?' He shook his head. 'Overnight he was richer by many hundreds of thousands of pounds,' Shelly explained, 'and immediately he resigned from his job and headed for a tax haven. Now he and Miriam live in a villa in Monte Carlo, with servants and a swimming pool and all the trappings. As she's so well catered for, Mrs Wilkins couldn't see the sense in Miriam having even more, and so she decided to make you her sole beneficiary. She was sure Harold would agree, because you and he had always got along so well together.'

David had been absorbing the details with grave interest. 'I'm to inherit *everything*?' he asked.

'The lot. So you see,' Shelly said hesitantly, 'the money Gail received could have been yours.'

'Mmm,' he agreed, deep in thought.

She made a play of brushing sand from her legs. If all of a sudden David had discovered he *did* give a damn, or two or three or twenty thousand, who could blame him? But where did that leave him and her? she wondered disconsolately.

'I'm fully aware that my gesture of coming out to Nevis makes a very small recompense,' she continued, with a sigh, 'but it was the only——'

'On the contrary, I reckon you've paid back the twenty grand in full. Think how much it would have cost if Jessica had gone to London or New York for treatment as I wanted her to,' he said, when Shelly made a protest. 'First there'd have been her air tickets, then, say, six or eight weeks in a hotel. Add specialists' fees, plus payments for drugs et cetera, and—there you are.'

She shook her head. 'No.'

'I'm a couple of thousand short?' His blue eyes sparkled. 'In that case I reckon I'm allowed to demand further payment.'

'What kind of payment?' she asked, not trusting his smile.

A muscular arm wrapped itself around her waist and he drew her down with him until his body was hard against hers and his weight pressed her into the sand.

'This kind,' he murmured.

'David,' she said, fighting against the drugging seduction of his nearness. She summoned up the will to push against his shoulders. 'David, I'm—I'm not so sure we should be doing this.'

He gave a muffled oath. 'Why the hell not?'

'Because—well, at the bungalow the morning after you did say you were worried about us becoming lovers and—and OK, you say you love me, but suppose you have second thoughts again?' she wailed.

'Sweetface, I was more than worried. To put it bluntly, I was scared to death,' he admitted, releasing her. 'Don't ask me why.' There was a pause. 'Yes, do.'

She sat up beside him. 'Why?'

He sighed. 'For more than two years my emotions hadn't had a single glimpse of daylight, yet there you were opening the window wide on things like caring and giving and——' David sighed again '—and being vulnerable to hurt. When you put your arms around me and made it plain how *you* felt, in a split second I realised I was in love with you, but I didn't like it. It seemed too spontaneous, too uncontrolled, too much the instant affinity.'

'Like Beatrice and Gail? And like——' she looked back over her shoulder '—you and Prince?'

'Exactly,' he said, seriously. 'I'd decided that if I ever did fall in love again—and it was a big *if*—it would be strictly on my terms. I intended to choose who, where, when. What I hadn't realised was that love doesn't bother about terms, schedules, being in the right place at the right time. It just erupts wherever and whenever. It breaks through barriers, crashes aside intentions, smashes resistances.'

Shelly grinned. 'That's what you couldn't handle?'

He nodded. 'All my insecurities ganged up on me. I thought of how Anneka had cut my self-esteem to ribbons, of how I'd sworn I'd never allow another woman to get close enough to hurt me again, and——' his shrug was diffident '—the cold sweats struck.'

'So when you said you didn't want anyone to get hurt, you were thinking about yourself?'

'No. Oh, I don't deny my own feelings were very much in my mind, but I did mean both of us.' He touched her cheek. 'The last thing I wanted was to cause you pain.'

'But you did!'

'I realised that straight away,' he said, frowning. 'But, as half of me was wanting to grab you tight and never let you go, the other half was wondering how, if, should, *could* I face up to how I felt?' David expelled a breath. 'I've explained my reaction over the painting, but I suspect there was another reason. At that moment I needed to put a wedge between us, so when it happened along I jumped on it. Does that make any kind of sense?'

'It does,' she nodded.

'Later, when you explained away our one-night stand by claiming to have been drunk, I tried to explain away what I'd felt when we'd made love. I put it down to a soaring of emotions after the flight. I was fooling myself,' he said drily. 'I've been around long enough to know you don't create that kind of ecstasy unless heart and body beat as one. I'd have given anything not to have gone with the Americans, to have had a chance for us to be together, to reconcile my feelings, to get used to everything. The only good aspect was that the trip gave me plenty of time to think. Which I did, long and hard and seriously.' David caressed the pulse which beat at her wrist. 'Will you marry me? If you do, I'll keep you safe from thunder and lightning, and falling coconuts.'

'Honest?'

'Cross my heart.'

Shelly laughed and wound her arms around his neck.

'Then yes, please.'

The laughing stopped and the kissing began. Mutual need drew them back on to the sand, mouth against eager mouth, limbs entwined.

'I love you,' David murmured, his kisses burning a path along the tendon from her ear down to the warm hollow in her throat.

'And I love you, too.'

He raised his hands to the straps of her swimsuit and eased them down until the material bunched around her waist. Once again she felt his touch on her breasts, the caress of the pad of his thumb against her nipples and, as he lowered his head, the in and out flicking of his tongue.

'How the hell I managed to stay so in control at the bungalow I'll never know, because now——' His eyes were dark and ardent. He was breathing hard. 'Have you ever made love in the open air?' David demanded.

'No.'

'Nor I,' he said, his gaze locked with hers.

Shelly wriggled, sliding the swimsuit over her hips and kicking it away.

'Darling,' she murmured, her breath mingling with his, 'there's always a first time.'

Coming Next Month

#1215 FRIEND OR FOE Jenny Arden
Kira's late husband had given Glenn Mason guardianship over her stepdaughter, Heather—a fact Kira deeply resents. But his responsibility certainly doesn't give Glenn any right to interfere in her life—and sparks fly when he tries!

#1216 LOVERS TOUCH Penny Jordan
The only way Eleanor de Tressail can keep her promise to her grandfather to keep the estate in the family is a marriage of convenience to wealthy Joss Wycliffe Only, for Eleanor, it is a case of love

#1217 NOT WITHOUT LOVE Roberta Leigh
Julia's assignment is a challenge—to guard an engineer-inventor who has received death threats. Since Rees Denton refuses to have a bodyguard, Julia has to operate undercover as his personal assistant. But how can she watch over him at night?

#1218 WILD JUSTICE Joanna Mansell
Cassandra has enough problems coping with her overly possessive father, so she is furious when Jared Sinclair lures her to his isolated Scottish home for reasons entirely different from those he's given her Surely it can't be just for revenge?

#1219 CHERISH THE FLAME Sandra Marton
Everyone's happy about Paige's forthcoming marriage to Alan Fowler—except his older brother, Quinn, who returns on the eve of the wedding. He tells Paige her father has been embezzling money from the Fowlers for years—and shocks her with the price for his silence!

#1220 THE DEVIL'S SHADOW Sally Wentworth
Her glamorous sister, Verity, spoiled Charlotte's early romance with Craig Bishop. Now, six years later, with Charlotte's dreams about to come true, Verity seems ready to do it again!

#1221 THE GATHERING DARKNESS Patricia Wilson
Nurse Julia Redford agrees to accompany her young patient Justine to her guardian's home in the Camargue. Julia has managed to cope with arrogant, overbearing Luc Marchal on her home ground, but once in France, Justine seems fine—and it's Luc who gives Julia problems!

#1222 BRAZILIAN FIRE Karen van der Zee
Chantal finds the sudden switch of life-styles from small-town America to the glamorous sophistication of Rio more than bewildering. She is even more puzzled by the cool, arrogant Enrico Chamberlain, who seems to hold her in such contempt!

Available in November wherever paperback books are sold, or through Harlequin Reader Service:

In the U.S.
901 Fuhrmann Blvd.
P.O. Box 1397
Buffalo, N.Y 14240-1397

In Canada
P.O Box 603
Fort Erie, Ontario
L2A 5X3

INDULGE A LITTLE SWEEPSTAKES

OFFICIAL RULES

SWEEPSTAKES RULES AND REGULATIONS. NO PURCHASE NECESSARY.

1. NO PURCHASE NECESSARY. To enter complete the official entry form and return with the invoice in the envelope provided. Or you may enter by printing your name, complete address and your daytime phone number on a 3 x 5 piece of paper. Include with your entry the hand printed words "Indulge A Little Sweepstakes." Mail your entry to: Indulge A Little Sweepstakes, P.O. Box 1397, Buffalo, NY 14269-1397. No mechanically reproduced entries accepted. Not responsible for late, lost, misdirected mail, or printing errors.

2. Three winners, one per month (Sept. 30, 1989, October 31, 1989 and November 30, 1989), will be selected in random drawings. All entries received prior to the drawing date will be eligible for that month's prize. This sweepstakes is under the supervision of MARDEN-KANE, INC. an independent judging organization whose decisions are final and binding. Winners will be notified by telephone and may be required to execute an affidavit of eligibility and release which must be returned within 14 days, or an alternate winner will be selected.

3. Prizes: 1st Grand Prize (1) a trip for two to Disneyworld in Orlando, Florida. Trip includes round trip air transportation, hotel accommodations for seven days and six nights, plus up to $700 expense money (ARV $3,500). 2nd Grand Prize (1) a seven-night Chandris Caribbean Cruise for two includes transportation from nearest major airport, accommodations, meals plus up to $1,000 in expense money (ARV $4,300). 3rd Grand Prize (1) a ten-day Hawaiian holiday for two includes round trip air transportation for two, hotel accommodations, sightseeing, plus up to $1,200 in spending money (ARV $7,700). All trips subject to availability and must be taken as outlined on the entry form.

4. Sweepstakes open to residents of the U.S. and Canada 18 years or older except employees and the families of Torstar Corp., its affiliates, subsidiaries and Marden-Kane, Inc. and all other agencies and persons connected with conducting this sweepstakes. All Federal, State and local laws and regulations apply. Void wherever prohibited or restricted by law. Taxes, if any are the sole responsibility of the prize winners. Canadian winners will be required to answer a skill testing question. Winners consent to the use of their name, photograph and/or likeness for publicity purposes without additional compensation

5. For a list of prize winners, send a stamped, self-addressed envelope to Indulge A Little Sweepstakes Winners, P.O. Box 701, Sayreville, NJ 08871.

DL-SWPS

INDULGE A LITTLE SWEEPSTAKES

OFFICIAL RULES

SWEEPSTAKES RULES AND REGULATIONS. NO PURCHASE NECESSARY.

1. NO PURCHASE NECESSARY. To enter complete the official entry form and return with the invoice in the envelope provided. Or you may enter by printing your name, complete address and your daytime phone number on a 3 x 5 piece of paper. Include with your entry the hand printed words "Indulge A Little Sweepstakes." Mail your entry to: Indulge A Little Sweepstakes, P.O. Box 1397, Buffalo, NY 14269-1397. No mechanically reproduced entries accepted. Not responsible for late, lost, misdirected mail, or printing errors.

2. Three winners, one per month (Sept. 30, 1989, October 31, 1989 and November 30, 1989), will be selected in random drawings. All entries received prior to the drawing date will be eligible for that month's prize. This sweepstakes is under the supervision of MARDEN-KANE, INC. an independent judging organization whose decisions are final and binding. Winners will be notified by telephone and may be required to execute an affidavit of eligibility and release which must be returned within 14 days, or an alternate winner will be selected.

3. Prizes: 1st Grand Prize (1) a trip for two to Disneyworld in Orlando, Florida. Trip includes round trip air transportation, hotel accommodations for seven days and six nights, plus up to $700 expense money (ARV $3,500). 2nd Grand Prize (1) a seven-night Chandris Caribbean Cruise for two includes transportation from nearest major airport, accommodations, meals plus up to $1,000 in expense money (ARV $4,300). 3rd Grand Prize (1) a ten-day Hawaiian holiday for two includes round trip air transportation for two, hotel accommodations, sightseeing, plus up to $1,200 in spending money (ARV $7,700). All trips subject to availability and must be taken as outlined on the entry form.

4. Sweepstakes open to residents of the U.S. and Canada 18 years or older except employees and the families of Torstar Corp., its affiliates, subsidiaries and Marden-Kane, Inc. and all other agencies and persons connected with conducting this sweepstakes. All Federal, State and local laws and regulations apply. Void wherever prohibited or restricted by law. Taxes, if any are the sole responsibility of the prize winners. Canadian winners will be required to answer a skill testing question. Winners consent to the use of their name, photograph and/or likeness for publicity purposes without additional compensation

5. For a list of prize winners, send a stamped, self-addressed envelope to Indulge A Little Sweepstakes Winners, P.O. Box 701, Sayreville, NJ 08871.

© 1989 HARLEQUIN ENTERPRISES LTD

DL-SWPS

INDULGE A LITTLE—WIN A LOT!

Summer of '89 Subscribers-Only Sweepstakes

OFFICIAL ENTRY FORM

This entry must be received by: Sept. 30, 1989
This month's winner will be notified by: October 7, 1989
Trip must be taken between: Nov. 7, 1989–Nov. 7, 1990

YES, I want to win the Walt Disney World® vacation for two! I understand the prize includes round-trip airfare, first-class hotel, and a daily allowance as revealed on the "Wallet" scratch-off card.

Name ______________________________

Address ______________________________

City ____________ State/Prov. ______ Zip/Postal Code ______

Daytime phone number ______________________________
Area code

Return entries with invoice in envelope provided. Each book in this shipment has two entry coupons—and the more coupons you enter, the better your chances of winning!

DINDL-1

INDULGE A LITTLE—WIN A LOT!

Summer of '89 Subscribers-Only Sweepstakes

OFFICIAL ENTRY FORM

This entry must be received by: Sept. 30, 1989
This month's winner will be notified by: October 7, 1989
Trip must be taken between: Nov. 7, 1989–Nov. 7, 1990

YES, I want to win the Walt Disney World® vacation for two! I understand the prize includes round-trip airfare, first-class hotel, and a daily allowance as revealed on the "Wallet" scratch-off card.

Name ______________________________

Address ______________________________

City ____________ State/Prov. ______ Zip/Postal Code ______

Daytime phone number ______________________________
Area code

Return entries with invoice in envelope provided. Each book in this shipment has two entry coupons—and the more coupons you enter, the better your chances of winning!

© 1989 HARLEQUIN ENTERPRISES LTD.

DINDL-1